One Desperate Life

A gripping thriller

D.J. Maughan

Hulyeseg Inc

For you, Loops. Thank you for your friendship and support. From the very beginning, when I expressed my desire to write, you supported and encouraged me. You'll never know how much that meant to me.

Prologue

Early in the morning of April 11, Joseph Taylor walked out the back door of his single-level farmhouse in Denver, Colorado, with purpose. A week earlier, he had purchased this plot of land from Ezekiel Hansen, who had inherited it from his father, Jedediah Hansen. Joseph was no stranger to hard work. He grew up on a farm, the youngest of four sons. His father, Henry Taylor, taught his boys the value of good, honest labor. Joseph remembered his father admonishing him, "Go to bed better than you left it."

The Taylor farm, on the other side of town, was one of the most prosperous in the county. Since Joseph was a teenager, he knew he wanted to follow in his father's footsteps. He craved the satisfaction that would come from working his own land. When Ezekiel made his land available for purchase, Joseph convinced his father to loan him enough money to finance what amount he hadn't already saved.

As he stood on the porch of the small farmhouse, he inhaled the crisp, clean air. *His* air. After milking the cow and feeding the chickens and pigs, he turned his attention to the day's task. A large oak tree stood in the middle of five acres of perfection. Fertile soil waiting to be tilled, planted, and harvested. Although the large oak long predated him, he knew it had to go. The task would be long and arduous, but necessary. No farmer worth his salt would leave a tree in the middle of his prime crop.

Joseph loaded his wagon with the necessary tools, including two axes, two spades, a chain, and a saw. He guided Macho, his mule, straining from the weight of the wagon, across his virgin field. When he reached the large tree, he surveyed the surrounding land, considering where he might start. An area a few paces from the tree stopped his search. The ground was void of vegetation. Odd for this time of year. As he examined it more closely, he found the soil had recently been disturbed. Not in the last few weeks but certainly since the previous fall. He gazed over the barren field and those surrounding it, wondering who might have been out here and why.

Curious, he walked back to his wagon and removed a spade. Gripping it in his hands, he stabbed the ground of the recently upturned dirt. Sure enough, the dirt moved easily. Far too easy for earth that had seen years of snow, rain, and heat. Something was buried here. For fifteen minutes, he worked. Scooping large shovels full of soil. Eventually, he felt a change in the surface. It wasn't a rock or even a tree root. The tip of the spade pierced something different, at first soft, then hard. He pulled back the dirt and examined the ground when his curiosity morphed into horror. There, lying in his large hole, was the unmistakable right hand of a woman.

Chapter 1
Michael

Michael stops midstride, feeling a change on the uneven ground. His last footfall felt squishy. With the steady rain, every step is spongier than normal on the usually hard-packed dirt road, but this was different. His boot slipped as it landed. Taking his eyes from the large stone building before him, he looks down and sees the source of the change. His boot rests in an enormous pile of fresh, wet horse manure. Cursing, he raises his leg and shakes his foot.

Michael resumes his stride and quickly reaches the opposite side of the street. He stops at a patch of grass and stomps his foot. He dances on the turf, rubbing the soles back and forth, hoping to eliminate the remaining droppings from his tread. Once satisfied, he looks back at the building, takes a deep breath, and ascends the stairs. After passing through the doors, he looks around, trying to orientate himself. A middle-aged man sits reading a newspaper behind a desk in the lobby. He lowers his paper, watching Michael. Finding he's been caught; he raises the paper, obscuring his eyes.

Michael walks toward him and stands beside the desk, clearing his throat.

"Excuse me, sir. I'm looking for the sheriff."

The man's face remains obscured by the paper. He gives no sign he heard Michael.

"Sir?"

The paper lowers, and the man with the spectacles looped around his ears frowns.

"I'm not the sheriff," he says, raising the paper.

Michael sighs. "I assumed. Do you know where I might find him?"

The man motions with his head toward the hallway. Michael thanks him and walks across the lobby and down the hall, wondering if everyone in Missouri is this pleasant. After clearing half the distance, he stops outside a solid door with a glass window with the words "Sheriff" stenciled in black lettering. Taking another deep breath, he steps to the door and knocks. Inside, he hears the shuffling of papers and the stomp of substantial feet. A shadow darkens the frosted glass, then the door swings open. A large, graying man stands before him, frowning.

"Yes?"

"Sheriff Winstanley?"

"Yes?"

"I need to speak with you, sir."

"What about?"

Michael's surprised to hear a thick Southern accent. Far more prominent than others he's heard since arriving.

"A prisoner you have in your jail. A man going by the name of Earnest Johns."

The sheriff furrows his brow and looks Michael up and down.

"What about him?"

"May I come in?"

The sheriff sighs and motions for Michael to enter.

The room is small, barely large enough to hold the desk that stands a few feet away. Michael has to step forward to allow room for the sheriff to close the door. Pulling a chair away from the wall, he positions it in front of the desk. He then walks around to the back of the desk and sits down, a small window behind him. He motions for Michael to sit.

Once Michael's seated, the sheriff asks, "What about Johns?"

Knowing the answer to the question, but asking anyway, Michael says, "Why are you holding him?"

The sheriff shakes his head. "Nope, that's not how this is going to work. You better get to explaining what brings you here—and fast."

Michael nods. "My name is Michael Delaney. I'm a detective with the Colorado police in Denver. I'm looking for a man who matches the description of Mr. Johns."

"Got an I.D.?"

Michael shows him his badge.

"What description?"

"Early thirties, dark hair, just over six feet tall. He's thin, with a scar under his chin and vibrant, blue eyes."

The sheriff raises an eyebrow and pulls a cigarette from a carton on his desk. He offers one to Michael, and Michael takes it. The sheriff hands him a matchbox, and Michael lights his cigarette and then gives the matchbox back to the sheriff. Once the sheriff has his cigarette smoldering, he leans back, puffing smoke into the air above his head.

"A man came to town a few days ago. He visited my office, much like you did. Claimed Johns stole money from him." He lowers his gaze and grins. "A lot of money. Claimed Johns's real name is Richard Amhurst, that he borrowed money from him and never paid it back, then skipped town."

The sheriff comes forward, bumps his cigarette along the edge of the ashtray on his desk, then leans back again.

"I knew of Johns. The mayor spoke highly of him. Said Johns was new to town. Came a few months back. Seemed to be a reputable businessperson from someplace back in Illinois. He planned to build a hotel here in downtown. The mayor was helping him arrange it."

The sheriff leans forward, puffs on his cigarette, and places a hand flat on his desk.

"Well, this man from someplace in Texas comes in claiming Johns isn't who he says he is. He says his real name is Richard Amhurst. Seemed like a load of bull to me, but I figured I better hear him out. He had some paperwork that looked legitimate, so I took him to see the mayor. After we examined his documents and talked to him for a while, we brought Johns in."

The sheriff smiles and waves a hand.

"Johns denied the whole thing. Said he'd never been to Austin or wherever the man was from. Said he was from Illinois. But the man was convinced he was Johns and produced a photograph. It was Johns, all right. I arrested him, and we've been holding Johns here until we figure out what to do with him."

"Can I speak to him?"

"Why? He owe you money too?"

"No, but we've been looking for someone who matches his description. We think it might be him."

"From Colorado?"

"Yes."

"Have a photograph?"

"No."

He shakes his head. "I doubt it's him then. Johns is from Texas. Before that, maybe Illinois. Doubt if he's ever even been to Colorado."

"Well, if it's all the same to you, I'd like to talk to him."

"Suit yourself. I'll take you down there. But it sounds like you're barking up the wrong tree."

The sheriff stands and opens the office door. Michael follows him out, and they walk back down the hallway. When they reach the lobby, the sheriff waves to the man seated at the desk, still reading the newspaper.

"Mornin', Ron."

"Sheriff."

Ron's gaze follows Michael as he and the sheriff reach a set of stairs and descend. When they reach the basement, a jailer sits dozing on a chair in front of a set of iron bars.

"Wake up, Frank. This feller is a detective from Colorado. He wants to talk to Johns."

Frank stands from his chair and rubs the sleep from his eyes. He pulls the ring of keys from his waist as he eyes Michael. He unlocks the bars and swings open the gate. He walks down a row of jail cells on either side, with Michael and the sheriff following. Michael notices most are empty, but occasionally he sees a body lying on a bed or a face staring back at him.

Frank finally stops at a cell at the end of the row and bangs on the bars with his keys. A man lies on the bed, his face obscured.

"Johns," the jailer calls out. "Someone here to see you."

Although he's lying on the bed, Michael can see the man is tall. His clothes are rumpled, and his dark hair is plastered to one side of his head. Keeping his gaze down, the man swings his legs off the bed, plants his feet on the ground, then stands. He walks toward the bars, finally looking up as he reaches them. The hairs on the back of Michael's neck stand on end. His heart rate quickens and his blood boils. He knows he's found the man he's been looking for.

Chapter 2
Michael

Michael Delaney looks down at the notepad in his hand and then back at the prisoner sitting across the table from him. They sit alone in a small consultation room in the bowels of the jail. The man wears shackles on his wrists. The bright blue eyes stare through him. His face is void of expression. Michael feels as if he's nothing more than a tree in a forest, not worth another glance. Stubble covers the prisoner's chin; his hair is disheveled. He has the look of a man who has fallen off life's highest pedestal and isn't ready to admit it.

"Mr. Johns, my name is Detective Delaney. I'm from Denver, Colorado. I'd like to ask you some questions. Would that be all right?"

Earnest Johns says nothing. His blue eyes remain still, unblinking. A calm, apathetic look on his face.

"Have you ever been to Denver, sir?"

Nothing. No response. The blue eyes stare straight ahead.

"Are you hard of hearing? Would it help if I wrote the question for you?"

A momentary grin plays at the corner of Johns's mouth, but he says nothing.

Michael tears off a sheet of paper from his notepad and leans over the table. He writes out the question and passes it to Johns. Johns doesn't pick it up. He doesn't even look at it. His eyes continue to look through Michael.

Michael sighs and leans back. He expected this. Everything he's learned about the man since beginning his investigation in Denver indicates he's cold and calculating, never giving in to emotion. That is if this man is who he thinks he is.

"I can see you aren't really interested in talking. That's okay. I'd still like to ask you about some things. Would that be all right?"

The blue eyes blink, and Michael takes that as an affirmation.

"Can I call you Earnest?"

No response.

Michael holds up his hands, palms facing the prisoner. "All right, Mr. Johns, it is. Where are you from?"

Nothing.

"A man from Austin, Texas, claims your real name isn't Earnest Johns, but Richard Amhurst. Is that true? Is your name Richard?"

The blue eyes stare back at him.

"I don't think that's true. I think your real name is Thomas Slater. Is that right? Is your real name Tommy?"

No response.

"I'm looking for a man who killed three people in Colorado. The thing is, the man looks just like you. Does the name Helen Covington mean anything to you?"

The prisoner stretches his arms above his head and yawns.

"How about Jerry and Bea Slater?"

He brings them back down, clanging on the table. He stares at Michael, expressionless.

Michael glares at him, then looks down at his notepad and reads the name. It's a shot in the dark, but what does Michael have to lose? He knows the name is coming out of left field.

"How about Barbara Amhurst?"

The reaction is so slight that had Michael not been watching him closely, he would have missed it. The prisoner's blue eyes momentarily darken, and the muscles of his face tighten. Michael feels a rush of excitement; something's different about that name.

Chapter 3

Louise

"Can't you hear her calling?" Barbara said as she pushed open the door to my bedroom. My older sister stood glaring at me. I ignored her as I went on staring at my reflection in the mirror. "Are you ready?"

I looked her in the face and rolled my eyes, then turned back to the mirror and brushed a single strand of my chestnut hair away from my face in an exaggeratedly slow motion. Barbara sighed, walked to me, and griped my elbow, digging her nails into my skin as she pulled me up.

"Why do you have to do this? You know how she is."

I wouldn't give her the satisfaction of showing pain.

"Why do you ask questions to which you already know the answer?"

Barbara glared at me and pushed me toward the door. I knew she worried about making our mother happy, but I didn't. We had plenty of time. I wanted to let Mother sweat a little. I strolled down the large hallway as if on a Sunday afternoon walk in the park. The only difference was my sister's hands pressed firmly into the small of my back, prodding me forward.

When we reached the staircase, our mother stood at the bottom of the stairs, a sour look on her face. *What else is new?*

"What took you so long? You know your father can't be late," she barked as we descended.

"Sorry, Mama," Barbara said, stepping around me and nearly flying down the stairs. I guess one stair at a time wasn't enough.

When Barbara reached the bottom, she stood still, knowing our mother's expectations. She looked as if she'd been called to a military inspection. Her arms were at her side, but she was smiling. She loved this. She loved being judged by Mother.

The fire in our mother's eyes dissipated as she appraised her favorite child. She said nothing, but the snarl that adorned her face left. Silence from Mother was tantamount to lavish praise.

"I knew violet would be the right choice for you," she said to Barbara. "It's perfect for your complexion."

Barbara curtsied as our mother's eyes left her and fell on me. Her countenance darkened. She clicked her tongue and shook her head as she examined me.

"I wish I could say the same for you, Louise. I told you yellow would wash you out. When will you ever listen to me? It does nothing to hide the width of your hips. The only silver lining, if there is one, is that it detracts attention from that rat's nest on your head."

I love to experiment with different hairstyles, and this was one I saw from another young woman at school. Rather than argue, I said nothing, keeping my expression blank. Leave it to my mother to give me a much-needed boost of self-confidence.

"Well...I guess it's only one night. Come along, girls, your father has brought the carriage around."

Barbara exited the front of the house, and I followed with mother trailing. We descended the stairs leading away from our plush, two-story home in the suburb of Oak Park near Chicago. Our father stood at the carriage holding open the door, waiting to assist each of us as we climbed inside. I sat next to Barbara, opposite our parents, as the driver flipped the reins.

We arrived home just this morning after a year away at school. Barbara had just completed her second year at Notre Dame with an emphasis on elementary education. It was my first year. I completed a general slate of courses with an eye toward literature. It was my first full year away from Mother, and there were aspects of it that were nothing short of glorious. Weeks upon weeks of choosing my own clothes, hairstyles, and diet. I only wished I was going back in the fall.

We hadn't always had this relationship, Mother and me. When I was younger, she was loving and supportive. I'm not sure what changed as I reached my teenage years.

The inside of the carriage was silent as we glided along the streets of Chicago. The clip-clop of the horse was the only sound as I looked out the window, aware of my mother's eyes on me. That could only mean one thing—she wasn't finished with her criticism. I considered jumping out the side of the carriage. I wasn't in the mood to hear it. But to be fair, was I ever? I could feel Barbara squirming beside me. She couldn't handle the tension. "Barbara the Pleaser" was what I called her. Finally, after several seconds of silence, I gave Mother what she wanted and looked at her. I didn't even try to hide my annoyance.

"Yes, Mother?"

Her icy gaze met mine, but she said nothing for a time. When the words finally exited her mouth, I was surprised they weren't a barrage of criticism.

"How was your freshman year in South Bend?"

I stared at her, unsure if this was a trick. "Fine," I said, wondering if she knew.

During the final week of school, I was called to the dean's office. After inviting me in, he glowered at me over his desk, his small glasses perched on the end of his nose, a paper in his hands.

"Something very serious has been brought to my attention. And, considering your family pedigree, I thought it proper you be told."

I sat rigid on the other side of the plush desk, knowing what he was referring to.

"Miss Clifford, I am officially notifying you that your behavior these last several weeks is outside the rules of this university. The latest infraction, plagiarism, is the final straw."

He watched me, and I could feel my cheeks burn. He handed the paper across the desk, and I took it. My hands trembled with rage as I read the title.

"That's your paper." He picked up another and extended it to me. "This one was submitted a day before."

I took it from his hands but didn't examine it. I didn't need to. I knew who did this.

"Your professor believes the other student wrote it and you copied it. Do you have anything to say?"

"Sir," I began fighting to control my voice. "I wrote this paper. The other is a fake."

He sighed. "Your professor said you'd claim it." He picked up another paper from his desk and slid it across to me. At the top of the page, the words *Rough Draft* were written in a hand I immediately recognized. "This paper was given to the professor by the other student claiming ownership of this work. It proves she wrote the paper, rather than you."

I looked up from the page. I was having trouble breathing.

"I'm sorry to inform you I have no choice but to expel you from the university."

The words hit me like a punch to the gut, and I felt as if I might faint.

"Because school is almost out for the year, we'll allow you to finish. But you won't be readmitted next year."

That was a week ago. Since returning home, school had been a subject I'd tried to avoid. I figured the less she knew about it, the better.

"Are you looking forward to your sophomore year?"

"Yes," I said, warily.

Long ago, I learned brief responses were the easiest way to deflect Mother's attention. If she started in on me, I'd answer in one-word replies until she moved on. I always wondered if she knew what I was doing or didn't care, but it always worked. We looked each other in the eye, the fatigue obvious on her face. She opened her mouth to say something else, but stopped and turned to Barbara.

"Barbara, how was your second year?"

Like always, Barbara welcomed the conversation. She smiled brightly, always eager to please. "Oh, Mama, I loved it. I can hardly wait to go back in the fall."

Mother smiled at her enthusiasm. "I'm glad to hear it. But don't be too anxious. You have three months at home. It will be nice to have you in the house again. All your father does is read the newspaper and talk about business."

She looked at my father, who could just as easily be riding in the carriage by himself with the amount of attention he paid to us. Even the mention of his name didn't rouse him from his thoughts.

"Mama?" Barbara asked, "What will we be seeing tonight?"

Our mother had always made education a top priority. Not just in the formal sense, although she certainly valued it. She wanted us well-versed in the arts and required we attend the theater, symphony, art showcases, and ballet. No surprise that our first day home had us going to the theater.

"Oh, did I not tell you? It's a play written by Oscar Wilde, *The Importance of Being Earnest*."

I was surprised, and my face must have shown it. I looked at her and wondered if she knew Oscar Wilde was one of my favorite authors. His book, *The Picture of Dorian Gray*, was my all-time favorite.

"It's supposed to be quite pleasing. Eliza Merriweather told me she laughed until her sides ached when she saw it."

In a flash, my emotions went from annoyance to elation. I turned back to the window and smiled. The night had morphed from a total loss to something pleasurable.

Mother went on talking to Barbara.

"I had lunch the other day with Elise McKenna. She asked about you."

Barbara shifted on the seat beside me.

"Her son, John, just completed his first year of law school."

I couldn't help the pleasure I felt inside as I turned away from the window and watched my sister's irritation.

Our mother looked at me, then back at Barbara, surely noticing the interchange. She was undeterred. She knew what was best for us in all things.

"Barbara, I know how you feel about him. And I grant you, he's not the most pleasing fellow around. But he comes from an excellent family, and he's got a mind for business. You could do worse, my child."

"John is very nice," Barbara said with little enthusiasm.

"You aren't getting any younger, dear. I was married for two years at your age. You're the oldest and must marry first. Poor Louise won't be able to marry until you do. And believe me, our work is cut out for us there. It's time you encourage his interest."

Barbara looked at me, and I couldn't help but smile. She turned back to Mother.

"Mother, what are you planning?"

Our mother, having been found out, absently rubbed at an invisible wrinkle in her dress.

"Mother?"

She finally looked up. "All I'm asking is you give him a chance. You're very lovely, and he so admires you."

"Is he coming tonight?"

She said nothing; she didn't have to.

"Sitting with us?" Barbara asked.

"Perhaps."

Twenty minutes later, we pulled up outside the Auditorium Theatre. Our father exited first, followed by Mother, Barbara, then me. We ascended the steps in order of importance. It was no surprise I was at the end. I knew my place.

After entering, our father greeted friends and business associates while our mother mingled with their wives. As expected, Barbara and I followed close behind, waiting to be introduced. I looked at the clock on the wall, anxiously waiting for the bell to call us to our seats.

Mother talked with a woman she knew, then introduced us. The woman nodded, her attention on Barbara. I'd always been the "other Clifford girl" looming in the shadows. Barbara was the model, the one who could be in an advertisement. She was taller, with long legs and a tiny waist. She looked most like our mother, even sharing the same light hair and green eyes. I was shorter, with wide hips and curves. My only feature that made other women jealous was my eyelashes, long and dark, matching my hair.

The woman asked Barbara about her studies, while I took the opportunity to survey the crowd of finely dressed men and women. I saw a handful of familiar faces, even if I couldn't place their names. Finally, my eyes were drawn to a tall, handsome man talking with my father. He was much younger, and although he was several feet away, I couldn't help but notice the depth of his blue eyes. They were captivating. He laughed at something my father said, and I noticed how white and straight his teeth were. I couldn't help the immediate attraction I felt toward him.

"And what about you, dear?"

I turned to see all three women looking at me expectantly.

"Pardon me?"

"Mrs. Thomas asked what you occupy yourself with. Are you in school as well?" Mother prodded.

"Yes, ma'am. I'm in school too."

"At the same university?"

"Yes, ma'am."

The woman nodded, waiting for me to say more, but finally realized I wouldn't and turned back to Barbara.

I stayed engaged in the conversation only long enough to feel confident it wouldn't swing back to me, then allowed my eyes to turn back to the handsome man with my father. But when my gaze returned to them, I was disappointed to see they were gone. I looked around, trying to find them, then turned back to the women. Beyond Mrs. Thomas, walking toward us, was my father and the attractive man.

The men halted when they reached us and waited for a pause in the conversation. When Mrs. Thomas finally stopped blabbering about her family in Indiana, he got Mother's attention.

"Marilyn, I want to introduce you to Mr. Charles Watson of Houston, Texas."

"How do you do, ma'am?"

Mr. Watson stepped forward and took our mother's hand, raising it to his lips. His blue eyes sparkled as he looked at her.

My mother's cheeks colored, and she took a step back as she appraised him.

"How do you do?"

Mr. Watson retreated a step, his eyes never wavering from hers. My father put a hand on Watson's shoulder and motioned with the other to us.

"These are my girls, Barbara and Louise."

Mr. Watson turned his attention to Barbara and repeated the same steps he had taken with our mother. After kissing her hand, he looked into her eyes, then took a sideways step toward me. He reached for my hand, and I offered it to him. He was so close I couldn't imagine it fitting between us as he raised it. His eyes felt as if they had penetrated my soul. As if he knew everything about me. His soft lips brushed against the back of my hand. He paused, allowing my skin to rest against his. His moist breath tickled my skin. His cologne tingled my nostrils. We stood there, looking at each other as if nobody else was in the room. My body radiated with electricity as it passed from hand to toe. Finally, he released his grasp and stepped back. My heart raced. I felt out of breath. I couldn't ever remember feeling that way. Having a man do that to me.

"It's a pleasure to meet you both," he said.

A bell rang and woke me from my trance. It was as if he'd cast some type of spell over me. The bell indicated we had five minutes to reach our seats before they closed the doors and wouldn't reopen them until intermission. All around, conversation stopped as people moved toward the auditorium.

"I invited Charles to sit in our box with us tonight," my father told my mother.

"How lovely," she said, smiling. "Let's be off then."

Our mother said goodbye to Mrs. Thomas, then led the group up the stairs to our customary box seats. When we arrived, we found one of the eight seats already filled. John McKenna stood as we entered. Nobody was surprised to see him, least of all Mother.

Ever the host, our mother greeted him and introduced him all around. He knew everyone, except Mr. Watson. The two men eyed each other curiously. Once introductions were complete, he stepped back and waited for instructions. Mother pointed to a seat in the corner.

"John, why don't you sit there? Louise will sit in the seat beside you."

John frowned and started to object. "Umm…"

She had turned away from him but snapped back, daring him to argue. With challenging eyes, she looked at him. "Yes, Mr. McKenna? You have something you want to say?"

The color drained from John's face, and he moved to the seat and sat down.

Mother looked at me next, then Barbara, and finally Mr. Watson. Her look said it all. She was not to be trifled with. I walked over and sat beside John.

"Mr. Watson, you sit on the other side here. And Barbara will sit with you."

They did as she asked, and almost on queue, the orchestra played their first notes. It was as if even they waited for her.

When I learned we'd be seeing a play written by the great Oscar Wilde, I was so pleased. The idea that anything would pull my attention from the stage was preposterous. But as I sat in the plush cushioned seat in our balcony box, I couldn't help my frequent glances at my sister and Mr. Watson. Countless times throughout our childhood, I'd felt envy for my older sister. But at that moment, the feeling was greater than any I could remember. Barbara was the accomplished one, the essence of what a twenty-year-old woman should be. But I never wanted to switch places with her. Never until that moment.

Chapter 4

Louise

"How did you girls like the play?" Mother asked, her face engulfed in shadow.

I sat beside Barbara, facing our parents, our backs to the front of the carriage. The sun had set while we were inside the theater.

"Oh, I loved it," said Barbara. "It was so funny."

"What about you, Louise?" Mother asked.

"Surprising..."

"How so?"

The voice was my father's. It turned out the play wasn't the only surprise of the night.

"Well...the novel was nothing like tonight's play."

"No?"

"No. Quite the opposite, actually. Tonight, we watched a lovers' comedy. Something light and jovial. Dorian Gray is anything but."

"What's it about?" Barbara asked, looking at me. Hers was the only face I could see.

"It's about a man who has a portrait painted of him. He meets Lord Henry Wolton, an aristocrat, and believes the only things that matter are beauty and sensual fulfillment. Dorian, realizing his beauty will someday fade, sells his soul. Instead of his physical body fading, his portrait does. He lives an amoral life, and the portrait shows each of his many sins."

The carriage went silent, other than the clip-clop of the horse. I watched Barbara, confusion in her eyes. My father uttered a low humph.

"So, it's not a comedy?" Barbara asked.

I chuckled. "No...far from it."

Barbara sat back.

After several seconds of nothing but clip-clop, my mother said, "Maybe what we saw tonight isn't all that different?"

Nobody responded, unsure what she meant.

"This Dorian Gray book sounds like it teaches a lesson. Does it not? The author wanted us to see that physical beauty fades. If that's all we are, we'll be unfulfilled. Our lives will be unfulfilled. Is that the lesson, Louise?"

I nodded but then realized they couldn't see me, so I said, "Yes, I think so."

"And what did we watch tonight? A play about two men pretending to be someone else? Living a lie to avoid their responsibilities. Both have an important message to teach. He just used a different vehicle to teach it."

We let her words sink in.

After a couple of minutes, Barbara said, "So, who was Earnest?"

I looked at her across the carriage, then back. "Huh?"

"Earnest. Who was he? Which man?"

"Uh...neither."

She shook her head. "But the play was called *The Importance of Being Earnest*. One of them had to be."

I looked at her and wondered how much of the conversation she'd understood.

"Barbara, what did Mother just say? Both men pretended to be Earnest. They were hiding who they really were."

We stared at each other with our parents silent across the carriage.

"Hmm," she said. "Do you think there are men like that?"

"Like what?" Mother asked.

"Pretending to be Earnest. Going by different names. Living different lives."

"Preposterous," Father said. "I don't see how anyone could do that in this day and age."

Barbara agreed. It was an interesting question, and I pondered it as I looked out the window, noticing the shadowed buildings as we passed. Was Father right? Was it preposterous? Or was it really possible?

Before long, we pulled up in front of our house. Father opened the door and paid the driver, then assisted each of us from the carriage. Mother walked up the steps first and was greeted by Betty, our housemaid. She held an envelope.

"A telegram came for you, ma'am."

Mother thanked her and took it, entering the house. Barbara and I followed her inside. We were exhausted, having come home from school that day. But a telegram wasn't a daily occurrence, and we were curious. We stood on either side of Mother, waiting as she opened it. Almost immediately, her hand flew to her mouth, and tears sprang to her eyes. A sob escaped her chest as she read.

Alarmed, we reached for her, and she crumpled into Barbara's embrace. My hands being free, I took the message from her and read it.

THE WESTERN UNION TELEGRAPH COMPANY

RECEIVED

317 WILSHIRE, CHICAGO, ILLINOIS

MARILYN CLIFFORD

REGRET TO INFORM YOU – (STOP) – SISTER EVELYN MURPHY AND HUSBAND ORVILLE MURPHY DROWNED AT SEA – (STOP) – PASSENGERS ON TITANIC

Chapter 5

Louise

It was several minutes since I had heard any voices, and I assumed it was safe to go down. I looked at myself one more time in the mirror, rose from the seat, and exited my bedroom. I walked down the hallway, intending to go downstairs, but stopped at the closed door midway down. Nibbles was awake and eager to leave the cage. I opened the door, closed it, and walked over. His cage stood by the window, and he loved to look out, seeing the other birds in the neighborhood.

"Good morning, Nibbles," I said, raising the black sheet that covered his cage.

"Hello, baby," he said back. That was one of his favorite phrases.

I unlocked the cage, and he climbed down from his perch and walked out. I extended my finger, and he stepped on, working his way up to my shoulder. He was a Quaker parrot, bright green and full of life. They call them Quakers because they shake their entire bodies when they get excited. He stood on my shoulder and leaned forward, touching his beak to my lips and making a kissing sound.

Birds had always fascinated me. When I was twelve, my parents gave him to me as a birthday gift. He was our family pet.

I played with him for twenty minutes, then gave him his food and water and went downstairs. As I descended, I listened for any movement. The house was silent, just as I had hoped. When I reached the kitchen, I didn't bother with the light switch. Enough light filtered through the windows, especially when I opened the curtains. I looked out on the two-acre lot we had behind the house. The sun was rising, and it looked like it was going to be a lovely spring day. The apple tree behind our house was full of pink blossoms, and I was tempted to go out and smell them.

But I knew I shouldn't. Emma Jameson would be waiting for me in the park. We had made plans to meet, and she always complained I was late. I hadn't seen her since I'd returned from school. I looked down at my watch and saw I still had thirty minutes. Good. If I snuck out now, I'd be able to avoid any conversation with my family.

After receiving the telegram last night about my uncle and aunt being killed aboard the *Titanic*, Barbara and I sat with our mother in the parlor trying to console her. It seemed no matter what either of us said, she was inconsolable. She was her only sister, like Barbara and me.

A couple of days ago, word spread about the sinking of a great ship in the Atlantic. Father talked about it when he came home from work. Never in our wildest dreams did we think we knew anyone aboard. While our relatives were in Europe and were due home soon, how many ships made that voyage every week? It was a shock to hear they were dead.

After trying for an hour to care for our grieving mother, I gave up and went to bed. As I climbed the steps to my room, a question kept repeating in my mind: Would I be that upset if Barbara died? The fact that I asked myself that unnerved me. She was my sister. Of course, I'd be upset. But I'd be lying if I said I'd be devastated like my mother was. The thought continued to trouble me as I lay in bed, staring at the ceiling. Tossing and turning, I asked myself question after question. How could Mother be so close to her sister? Didn't she feel any of the same annoyances I felt? Did aging change their relationship? Why didn't I feel that same affection for Barbara? An hour went by before I finally fell asleep.

I turned from the window and stepped lightly to the pantry. Thinking about the day ahead made me hungry. I knew I'd be with Emma for hours and didn't know when I'd next have occasion to eat. Emma was like Barbara. She seemed to gain nutrients from the sun. A glass of sunshine could fill her for hours.

I opened the pantry and looked at the shelves. I planned to get myself toast with butter, but a box of something called Post Toasties stopped me. The box featured a woman holding an overflowing bowl in her hands. Inside the bowl was what I assumed to be Post Toasties. I picked up the box, looked inside, and pulled one out. I examined it, then looked back at the box.

I heard a throat clearing behind me.

I whirled around to see my mother sitting at the kitchen table. She stared at me, her hair pulled up in a bun, her eyes bloodshot. My heart sank. I knew I'd spent too much time stalling.

"You put them in a bowl and pour milk over them," she said, motioning with her hand.

"Are they good?"

"I don't think so. But your father likes them. Try some."

I got a bowl and spoon from the cupboard and poured some of the Post Toasties, then sat across the table from my mother.

"Did you want some?"

"No," my mother said, waving her hand.

"I thought you were still in bed. You were up late."

"I couldn't sleep. Your father left for work, and I stayed here."

I didn't know what to say, so I dunked a spoon into the toasties and took a bite. They crunched under my teeth. After several chews, I tasted nothing. They were bland and seemed like what sawdust might taste like. I grimaced and wanted to spit them out, but I knew the wrath that would come my way if I did. *Ladies don't spit*. I chewed several more times, then swallowed, forcing them down.

She'd been watching me and could see my distaste. "Your father lets them sit for a couple of minutes in the milk. He says it makes them soft."

That might be true, but I knew no amount of softening was going to change the taste. I sat there, wondering what I was going to do. She'd never let me throw them out, and I had taken too many. An idea struck, and I stood from the table. I walked back to the pantry, picked up the sugar tin, and sat back down. I never looked up, knowing my mother was watching. I covered the toasties with sugar, stirred them, and took another spoonful. This time, they were almost good. I knew I'd be able to finish. I looked up to see my mother's disapproving look.

"Yes?" I asked.

"Does everything need to be so sweet?"

"I like sweet."

She shook her head and looked away. I knew she wanted to say something but was holding back. I don't know why, but I pressed.

"What?"

"Have you ever thought maybe you eat too much sweet? Maybe that's why…"

"Maybe that's why what, Mother?"

I could see she was debating whether to go on.

"Maybe that's why you have extra weight."

I knew better. I'd baited her into it. For once, she actually held her tongue, but I couldn't let it go. It was as if I wanted to hear it. Like by her saying it, I could justify my own thoughts. I could tell myself that no matter what I did, it was never good enough. She only wanted to control me. Even what I ate and looked like.

I shook my head, grabbed the sugar, and sprinkled more into the bowl. I took a bite, and our eyes met. As I chewed, I regretted my actions. It was way too sweet. Maybe even worse than none at all, but I would not tell her that. I couldn't give her the satisfaction. As if that wasn't enough, I swallowed, took another bite, and exhaled an exaggerated "mmm."

She shook her head and muttered, "You're just like your aunt."

"Evelyn?"

"Yes."

This was my first time hearing the comparison, and it surprised me.

"I thought you liked Evelyn?"

She frowned. "I loved her."

"Then why compare her to me?"

She glared at me. "What are you talking about?"

"Nothing," I said, dunking my spoon back in the bowl and raising it to my mouth. Not only was it too sweet now, but it went from too hard to mush in an instant. For the first time, my pride might have met its match.

A buzz at the door saved me. I was fully dressed, and she was wearing a robe over her pajamas. A lady was never seen in public that way.

"Louise, will you get it?"

I nodded and walked to the entrance. When I opened the door, a young man near my age stood looking down at me. He held a beautiful bouquet.

"Clifford residence?" he asked.

"Yes."

He thrust the flowers into my arms and gave me a note to accompany them. I turned the note over and was surprised and a little disappointed to see the name on the envelope. I thanked him and walked back to the kitchen.

"Who was that?" Mother asked before I rounded the corner. When she saw me, her eyebrows rose in surprise.

I set the flowers on the table and handed her the note. "They're for you."

She opened the envelope and read the note aloud.

Mrs. Clifford,

I'm sorry for your loss. Please accept these flowers as a condolence at such a difficult time for you and your family.

Sincerely,

Mr. Charles Watson

She looked up at me, and I knew we were both thinking the same thing.

"He must really like Barbara."

Chapter 6

Louise

I knocked on the door to my sister's bedroom but didn't wait for her to respond. Barbara stood in front of the full-length mirror, smoothing the red dress she had on. A red bow was in her hair, and it accented her dress perfectly. Like always, her fashion sense was unmatched. I walked over and looked at myself in the mirror standing next to her, feeling a stab of self-doubt.

"Are you ready?" I asked.

"I don't know," she said, frowning in the mirror. "Is this dress right? Should I change?"

I told myself not to roll my eyes as I analyzed the pair of us in the mirror. She looked perfect. Barbara was the type of girl who could try on anything and make it look better than on the store mannequin. I didn't look bad, but it wasn't a fair comparison.

"You look amazing. He won't be able to keep his eyes off you."

She looked at me with a grateful smile. She probably thought I was telling her what she wanted to hear, but it was the truth. I wasn't that nice. Seeing us side by side assured me I couldn't compete. The confidence I felt as I closed my bedroom door and walked down the hall had flown out the closed window.

Strangely enough, I found it a relief. This afternoon, as I sat in my bedroom daydreaming about Charles and what it might be like to be with him, I grew nervous. I convinced myself that somehow, he would see me instead of Barbara. That I'd be the sister he'd want to court. After seeing myself next to her, I saw it for what it was—a little girl's fantasy.

When Barbara reached up to adjust the bow in her hair, I saw her hand tremor, and it gave me pause. It was the first time I ever remembered seeing her show nerves. Ever! I realized I wasn't the only one putting expectations on myself. A surge of empathy rose from my gut, and I reached over to help her. Seeing it wasn't perfect, but knowing it never would be for her, I gripped her hand and pulled her toward the door.

"Come on. Mother won't be happy if we're not there when he arrives."

We held hands, walking down the hallway, and something about feeling her shake made me see the entire night differently. I wanted to help her.

"You look gorgeous. He'd be blind not to see it."

"Thank you," she whispered. "Go first, would you?"

I looked at her and saw what she meant. She wasn't talking about the stairs. She'd always been the first to stand for Mother's inspections. The first introduced. The first to talk. The model to be presented. How exhausting that must have been. For the first time, I saw it. I hated to be compared to her, but she carried the weight of expectation. Maybe that was worse.

That night, she was asking to switch places with me. She'd pleaded with her eyes for me to lead. To be the first to greet Charles. To take the pressure off her. I couldn't help the surprise and uncertainty I felt, but I told her I would as we descended the stairs.

"It's about time, ladies," Mother said as we arrived at the bottom.

We stood side by side as Mother approached. We had done this ritual thousands of times, but this time, it was different. Mother looked at Barbara first, and although she didn't say it, I could see she was pleased. Her eyes smiled with delight. Barbara beamed at her as only she could, and Mother turned her attention to me.

"I like that dress, Louise. I've always told you dark colors are slimming. I'm pleased to see you're finally listening."

A horse neighed outside, demanding our attention, and Mother went to the window. She looked out, nodded, and then came back more serious than before.

"They're here. Line up."

In unison, we turned, straightened, and smiled. We could do that in our sleep. As long as I could remember, we'd entertained Father's business guests in our home. Mother had specific expectations about how we should stand, act, and speak. Barbara always stood to Mother's left, then me beside her. That's how we were when the sound of heavy feet thumped up the stairs and stopped as Father pushed open the door and stepped inside. Behind him followed Charles. He was wearing a dark suit, a white shirt, and a light blue tie. The tie matched his eyes, which I found alluring. He smiled a toothy smile, swept off his hat, and bowed. Our father put a hand on his shoulder and walked him toward our mother.

"Charles, you remember my wife, Mrs. Clifford?"

"Thank you for the invitation, ma'am."

He stepped forward and took my mother's hand, kissing it and looking into her eyes. I'd never seen any man have that effect on her. She actually blushed before thanking him for the flowers.

"Oh, it's the least I could do. I'm sorry for your loss."

"Thank you."

"You remember my daughters?"

Mother turned, then stopped, momentarily caught off guard. I was standing beside her, rather than Barbara. Seamlessly, we had switched places, knowing her focus would be on Charles. Anger flashed in her eyes, but she regained her composure, and only those who knew her best would have seen it. She extended her hand to me and smiled up at him. "My younger daughter, Louise."

He stepped forward, took my hand, and looked deep into my eyes, just like before. Once again, I felt a shiver run down my spine as his lips brushed my skin.

He released my hand as Mother introduced Barbara. Barbara blushed as he took her hand and kissed it.

"Nice to see you again, Barbara."

She smiled.

Mother led him down the hall to the dining room, with the three of us following close behind. After entering, she pointed out our seats. Mother and Father sat in their customary places on either end of the table. Barbara and I were seated on one side, and Charles on the other.

After Betty served our first course, Mother asked Charles about his home in Houston. Father joined in the conversation, and as was customary, Barbara and I sat listening. Often, I found the conversations tedious and boring when a business associate of Father's would come. But this time, the man across the table captivated me. Not only was he incredibly handsome, but he was charismatic, intelligent, and confident. He had the three of us eating from the palm of his hand all night.

At one point, Mother went to the kitchen to speak with our cook, and Father left to fill his drink. They were only gone seconds, but Charles turned his gaze in my direction. There we sat, staring at each other. When Mother reentered, I looked away, but I could see Charles did not. It wasn't until Father handed him a drink that he stopped his penetrating stare. For the rest of the evening, he didn't look at me again, and I started to think I'd imagined the whole thing.

As the evening wound down, we escorted Charles to the door. He said good-night to each of us, then walked out with Father. The three of us stood in the entrance while the men said goodbye and Charles climbed into a coach. When Father returned, he smiled at Mother.

"Your dreams have come true."

"Why?" she asked.

"Oh, you know very well. You've been angling for him to court Barbara, and he just asked for my permission."

Mother clapped and laughed in joy. Barbara beamed. And I felt as if I'd been kicked in the gut by a horse. Though I shouldn't have been surprised. Yet, I was. Mother hugged Barbara, and Father went down the hall to his drawing room.

"Congratulations, Barbara," I said, and I meant it. I walked past her and up the stairs.

After putting Nibbles to bed, I reached my bedroom and shut the door. I removed my shoes and undressed. Downstairs, I could hear the joy in my family's voices. I imagined they'd be engaged before the summer was over. Barbara wouldn't be pushed into marrying John. And, like always, everything would be perfect for Barbara. Hers was a life truly blessed.

I, on the other hand, had a life truly cursed, as shown by my first year in college. Beginning with the very first lecture, I abhorred my pompous English professor, Dr. Hamby. Being new to the school, and not wanting to make waves, I sat along with the other freshman, as he made sexist remarks against women. I'd look around the room and wonder if anyone would stand up to him, but nobody ever did. I could see from their cast-down eyes, they were as uncomfortable as I was. One day, after several months, I could take it no longer.

We were reading *The Scarlett Letter* by Nathaniel Hawthorne. Dr. Hamby was discussing the literary qualities of the book and implied Hester Prynne, the main character, deserved to die rather than wear the letter A for the adultery she committed. Without raising my hand, I spoke up.

"And I suppose you also believe the Salem witch trials were God's work."

I could feel every eye in the room staring at me as I glared at him. His gaze fell upon me, but he never responded and went on with the lecture. It wasn't the last time I spoke against him in class, and our mutual disdain only grew. My grades suffered, and when that wasn't enough for him, he conspired with my roommate to have me accused of plagiarism and expelled from the university.

It was another sign that I couldn't overcome fate. I might as well be wearing a letter on my chest. Luck was never on my side.

That's why I knew I would never meet a man like Charles again. I would likely settle for some man my mother had arranged. Maybe John. At social functions, I'd be forced to see them together. To nod and smile and act so happy for them. All the while longing for the life I should have had.

I pulled back the covers and plopped down on the bed when a paper dropped to the floor. Curious, I bent over and picked it up. It was folded in thirds, and my name adorned the outside. I recognized the handwriting immediately, and my heart leaped. It matched the note with the flowers. I unfolded it and read the message: *Meet me in Wilmington Park under the large tree tomorrow at 3 pm.*

It was unsigned, but it didn't need to be. I knew exactly who wrote it. But how? How had he delivered it? How did he know which bedroom was mine? Then a thought gripped me. What if it wasn't intended for me? What if this note was for Barbara?

I turned it back over and saw my name again written on the outside. It *was* for me. I didn't imagine the way he looked at me across the table. It was real.

I laid back on the bed and held the note up to the light, rereading it. He wanted to meet me and didn't want anyone else to know. But why?

Chapter 7

Michael

After asking several more questions about Barbara Amhurst without a response or reaction, Michael gives up and calls for the guard. He walks up the stairs, down the hall, and stands outside the sheriff's office. He knocks, and after a few seconds, the sheriff opens the door, a cigarette dangling from his mouth.

"Get what you needed?" Sheriff Winstanley asks.

Michael shakes his head. "Nope. He won't say a word."

The sheriff nods and smiles.

"You knew?"

"I assumed."

"Why didn't you tell me?"

"Why should I? I hoped maybe you Denver folks would have a way to make him talk." "You said a man came here from Texas. Called him by another name."

"Right."

"Is that man here? Can I talk to him?"

"Nope. He went back to Texas."

"You said he proved to you he was this, Richard Amhurst. How'd he do that?"

"A photograph."

"Right, he had a photograph of Johns, correct?"

The sheriff crosses his arms and nods. "Also had loan documents. We compared the writing with the documents the mayor had. They matched up."

"Can I see those documents?"

"Nope. Don't have them. The mayor kept them."

Michael nods. "Where can I find the mayor?"

Chapter 8

Louise

I sat on the park bench, gazing at the large elm tree in the park's corner. I had arrived fifteen minutes ago but didn't go to the tree mentioned in the note. Instead, I sat on the bench, watching and waiting, thinking maybe the whole thing was a hoax or a game.

After learning he had asked permission from my father to court Barbara, I wrote off any chance of being with him. But reading that note last night, everything changed. I couldn't contain my excitement. Lying in bed, thinking about him, my excitement gave way to curiosity and anxiety. Why was he requesting to meet me? And why the secret note?

I pulled my fingers away from my mouth and sat on my hands. I was biting them again. You would think with all the chastening Mother had directed my way about the act, I wouldn't do it. But somehow my subconscious mind ached to disobey. If she saw me, I'd be reprimanded. I was already on thin ice with her. She and Barbara were shopping in the city, and I was supposed to go along. Mother wanted to run errands before our departure to New York City and her sister's funeral. She had expected Barbara and me to accompany her, and normally I'd go, but the note changed everything. I told her I couldn't, after agreeing earlier. I said I had plans with Emma. I expected her to be annoyed, but she was downright angry. She demanded I cancel, and only a crying fit was enough to make her relent. There was no way I wasn't going to the park. But, looking at the tree, it appeared to be for naught.

I looked back across the park and wondered if I was being watched. Maybe he was doing the same thing as me? Maybe he was testing me, seeing if I would go to the tree. I stood then and walked to it. Standing under it, I realized I should have been there the whole time. It was much cooler than the bench in the sun. I looked around, asking myself for the hundredth time what I was doing there, when a movement on the other side of the park caught my gaze. I held my breath as I watched him turn in my direction.

He was wearing a brown suit with a matching vest and tie. His hat completed the ensemble. His head was down as he walked, and he didn't look at me until he reached the tree. I expected him to stop several feet away, but he didn't, coming right next to me. Far too close for social standards.

"Sorry I'm late," he said so close I could feel his breath. "I underestimated how long it would take to get here."

I looked up at him, a sly smile on his lips.

"That's okay."

"No," he said, taking a step closer, "I didn't intend to make you wait."

I looked at him, wondering who he was. Everything about this meeting was improper, and he didn't seem to care. Butterflies tingled in my chest, and I had to remind myself to breathe. I knew I was blushing, but I couldn't help it. I wanted to say something. Anything. But what? I wasn't accustomed to speaking with men my age or just a bit older. Especially men like him. Seeing my discomfort, he stepped back and removed his hat, holding it in his hands. He looked at me the same way as last night. As if he wanted something. The intensity of his eyes both excited and worried me. I grasped for something to say.

"I wasn't sure who wrote the note."

He smiled and shook his head, but his eyes were still on me, watching.

"You knew who left the note."

He said it so confidently. Like there wasn't a question. *Who talks this way?* I barely knew the man. I knew I should back away, tell him the meeting was inappropriate, and leave. But my back remained glued to the bark of the tree. The excitement of the encounter overwhelmed me. I felt myself blushing furiously under his penetrating stare, but I was powerless to stop.

"Why did you want to see me?"

It was the question I'd been dying to ask, but now that it was out there, I was afraid to hear his response.

He raised an eyebrow. "You don't know?"

Is he playing with me?

"Barbara?"

He frowned. "What about her?"

"You want to talk about her?"

He chuckled. "If I wanted to know about Barbara, wouldn't I talk to Barbara?"

His response confused me. "But you asked my father…"

For the first time, he looked away from me and out at the park. I worried I was losing him. That I was doing something wrong.

"I told your father what he wanted to hear. He wants me to court Barbara, and I want him to loan me money. I'll feign interest in her until he gives me the loan."

He said it so nonchalantly. Why would he admit that to me?

He turned back and looked into my eyes, stepping closer again. He was inches from me. So close I thought my chest might graze his shirt. I swallowed, smelling his cologne. Unsure what to do but wanting an answer, I tried again, asking the same question, afraid of the answer for an entirely different reason.

"Why did you want to see me?"

He stared into my eyes, and I thought he might try to kiss me. I hoped he would, but knew he shouldn't.

"I think you know. Do I need to come right out and say it?"

I shook my head, looking into his eyes, wondering how I could possibly leave and go to New York.

Chapter 9

Louise

The carriage stopped at Grand Central Station, and Father exited, paid a man to carry our luggage, and assisted each of us from the carriage. I could feel my heart race with excitement. I'd never been on a train before. Mother and Father had several times, but they always left us girls home. Even our journey to college and back was on a stagecoach. After meeting Charles in the park, I'd seen him twice. Both times in public. Neither allowed us an occasion to speak. I kept hoping he would slip me another note. But he didn't, and now I was leaving.

Barbara and I walked behind our parents. Our father guided the procession. Two men walked behind us, pushing carts full of luggage. We entered the station, and the smell transformed from horse to machine. Smoke from the locomotives filled the air, and I found my breathing shallower. Each breath seemed less productive than the last, exasperated by the speed of our gait. I worried it might be like that on the train as well. Chicago to New York City could have been a nightmare.

My pace slowed as I stared at the large train before me. I marveled at the size and wondered at its approximate weight. I let the machine dominate my thoughts, forgetting my breath. I wondered how much force would be needed to move such a large object. I was confused about how a coal stove could create such a reaction.

"Louise," my father scolded, "keep up!"

I didn't realize I had fallen behind. A mass of humanity surrounded us, but I could see his head over the sea of people. All around me, people jockeyed for position, climbing aboard or forming lines eager for their turn. Most had bags and awkwardly fumbled up the stairs, trying to manage the load. Father walked us past the scores of humans to the front of the train. We followed him like a flock of sheep trailing a shepherd. A man in a uniform stood beside the front passenger car and smiled as we approached. This area, the first class, was far less chaotic.

"Do you have a ticket, sir?" he asked, tipping his cap.

My father reached inside his jacket and withdrew four tickets. The man took them, welcomed us aboard, and showed us to our compartment. Barbara and I shared a space, while our parents had one across the hall. Another uniformed man joined the first and opened the compartment door while the first stayed with our parents.

"Here you are, ladies," he said, ushering us in.

The space was compact. It was furnished with a bench seat, a bed stacked on another bed, and a small desk with a mirror above. Both beds were made up with blankets and pillows.

"Your bags will be along shortly. My name is Lester. I'll be your attendant for this trip. I'm here to assist in any way I can."

Barbara looked around the room and asked, "Lester, where is the powder room?"

Lester led us down the hall, past our parents' room, and pointed.

"We have several, miss. But the closest is midway down on the right, just before the dining car."

We thanked him, and he left. Five minutes later, the same men who had transported our bags arrived. I never realized they had split from us somewhere along the journey. Barbara began unpacking and arranging things while I sat on the bed. After a couple of minutes, she gave me a look.

"Yes?"

"Who says you get that bed?"

"Who says I don't?"

"I'm the oldest, and I get to choose."

I shook my head and laughed. "That only works when Mother is around." I exaggerated a search around the compartment. "Hmm, I don't see her here."

Barbara glared at me then, seeing I would not give in, she shrugged and walked to the window. "Fine, I want the top anyway."

A whistle sounded, and the train began to move. I joined Barbara at the window, and we anxiously watched as the train cleared the station and moved out of the city. I was surprised by how smoothly the huge locomotive moved. Compared to a carriage or automobile, the train effortlessly glided forward. I didn't feel any of the instability I was expecting.

Five minutes passed, and a knock sounded at the door. I opened it to find Mother.

"Your father has reserved us a table in the dining car. Come along."

We gathered our things and trailed behind as she guided us down the hallway. A woman passed in the other direction, and we had to stop and press ourselves to the walls. The tightness of the quarters was something we'd need to get used to.

When we reached the dining car, Mother gave her name to the attendant who greeted us, and he walked us past rows of tables. The car was bustling with activity. Servers and attendants hustled back and forth, caring for their guests. The attendant reached our table and pulled out a chair for Mother. I stood waiting my turn with Barbara at my side. Pleasure filled my veins as I watched the man who stood next to my father. Charles was on the train.

Chapter 10

Louise

After dinner we sat in the drawing car socializing, having drinks, and relaxing. Eventually, we returned to our sleeping compartments for the night. Several times during the meal, and afterward, I caught Charles staring at me. Our eyes would lock, and then I'd look away. I wondered if he could see my anger. I was happy that he was aboard, more than he could know. But what angered me was that he didn't tell me. Nobody had.

When we sat down to dinner, it was obvious everyone knew he'd be there, except for me. I looked at the faces of my family. None registered surprise. I learned he was going with us all the way to New York City. Father would introduce him to people who could help him with his business. It made sense, and I was pleased, but why didn't Charles tell me? He could have slipped me a note. He did before.

I wasn't angry that Father knew. Of course he would. He had arranged it. It didn't even bother me that Mother knew and didn't tell me. Why would she? But Barbara? Why would she know before me? Yes, he was formally courting her. But he didn't even like Barbara. It made me wonder if there was more to the story than I knew. Maybe Father had told her. But I couldn't believe she wouldn't have mentioned it to me, even in passing.

What angered me, what really made me upset, was that I had nearly tried to remove myself from the trip entirely. I wanted so badly to stay near him that I would have skipped my relatives' funeral just to see him. Mother never would have forgiven me. I would have risked so much for him, yet here he was on the train without even bothering to mention it to me.

Barbara opened the door to our compartment and entered, carrying her toiletry bag. I looked up from my book.

"Aren't you going to get ready for bed?" she asked.

I ignored her and went on reading. She shuffled around the compartment, putting things away, then shut off the light and walked past me to the ladder leading to her bunk.

"Hey?" I said.

"Hey, what?"

"Why'd you turn the light out?"

"Because I'm going to sleep, and I can't sleep with it on."

I saw the sag of the bed above me and wondered how weak the springs must have been if her skeleton frame could make it sag. I heard the creak and groan of the frame as she shuffled around. Then it was quiet, and I considered putting aside my book, grabbing my toiletry bag, and getting ready for bed. But I didn't want to. I was at such a good point in the story, and I wanted to know what happened next.

I swung my legs off the bed, went to the door, and exited. I looked down the hallway and noticed the lights were dim. But I could see lights remained at full brightness in the drawing room. I walked to the end of the hall, peeked inside the window of the door, and saw the room was empty. Perfect. I entered the car, found a spot tucked away in the corner with plenty of light, and sat down.

For twenty minutes I read undisturbed, lost in the heroine's plight, when I heard a door open behind me. I turned to see who it was, expecting a train attendant. My breath caught as our eyes met. Charles had entered, and he was coming to me. Not bothering to receive an invitation, he sat down across from me. His eyes never wavered. He was still wearing the navy blue suit he wore during dinner. The color made his eyes darker and more mysterious.

"I was looking for you," he said.

The comment excited me, but I was still angry about not being told he'd be traveling with us. I kept my voice cool, apathetic.

"Why?"

He raised an eyebrow. "Games, Louise?"

I didn't know why; he was never anything but bold, but his brashness again surprised me. All night, he never said boo to me. He would stare but never speak. Now he addressed me like we were, what, lovers? My confusion deepened under his watchful gaze, and I attempted to regain my footing.

"Why didn't you tell me you were coming with us to New York City?"

He grinned. "Jealous?"

I knew I was blushing, and I looked down at my book. But I told myself not to let him have the upper hand and glanced back up almost immediately. He laughed a boisterous laugh, and I looked around, worrying someone would hear. It was improper for us to be sitting there together late at night. A point he was oblivious to or careless of.

"Well, you shouldn't be," he said.

"What?"

"Jealous. You shouldn't be. I'm not interested in Barbara."

"No? You could have fooled me the way you talk to her."

He waved a hand. "An act. I'm giving your father what he wants. Once I have what I want, my intentions will be known."

"And what are those?"

He stared into my eyes. Then, without standing, he crossed the distance between us and sat beside me.

"You're the sister I want."

His statement both pleased and surprised me. Sitting here, so close to him, his eyes on me, I couldn't believe how much I longed for him. I wanted him to kiss me.

"You shouldn't talk like that," I said, not really believing it but feeling like I had to say it.

"Why? It's the truth."

Behind us, I heard the turn of a door handle, and fear jolted me. I stood from the seat and looked behind us. A train attendant entered. He glanced at me, then at Charles, then back to me. He carried a bag of something and walked down the aisle toward us.

"Is everything okay, miss?"

I wanted him to leave and also knew I was blushing furiously.

"Yes. I was here reading my book, then Mr. Watson happened upon me, and we chatted for a moment. I'm headed to bed now."

He eyed me closely, then looked at Charles. Charles nodded, and the man nodded back and continued on his way. He glanced at us one last time before exiting the other side of the car.

"I should head off to bed," I said to Charles, worried the attendant would tell my mother and father.

Charles stood and came toward me. He put his hands around my waist and pulled me to him. I couldn't believe the gall of this man. He was absolutely fearless, and I loved it. He leaned down and pressed his lips to mine. I was so stunned my eyes remained open but unfocused. After a moment, they shut, and I was overwhelmed with pleasure. His kiss was everything I had hoped for, and more.

After several seconds, he pulled away and looked into my eyes.

"I'm in compartment seven. I'll be waiting for you."

He pushed past me and walked back toward the sleeping car. I watched him go, admiring his back. When he closed the door, I stumbled to the powder room. Once inside, I stood over the sink and stared at my reflection in the mirror. *Did that really happen?* He kissed me. He invited me to his room. To his bed. The invitation was undeniable. *How could he do that?* I knew I couldn't go. I wasn't that girl. Women my age didn't visit single men in their cabins. I inhaled, reaching my fingers up to brush my lips. The motion brought the remembrance of his lips on mine. His body pressed against my body.

I don't know how long I stood there debating, staring at myself. Finally, somebody tugged on the door and pulled me from my daydream. I waited a minute, then exited, spotting a woman standing across the hall, waiting. We nodded to each other, and I made my way to the sleeping compartment. I walked past number eight on my way to number three, my compartment. I stopped, retraced my steps, and looked to my left. There, on the door, was the number seven. I stood before his door. Almost instantly, it opened, and Charles stood looking at me. I looked down the hall, then back to him, and stepped inside.

Chapter 11

Michael

Michael walks up the steps of the city hall in Kansas City, Missouri, and enters. When the day started, he couldn't have imagined he'd be in two different city halls on the same day in two different states. Before arriving in Kansas City, he didn't know the city was split between the two states. He always assumed Kansas City belonged to the state of Kansas. He asked a man on the street for directions to the city hall. The response confused him.

"Which one?" the man had asked.

"Excuse me?"

"Which city hall? Kansas or Missouri?"

Michael shook his head, thinking the man was daft. "Kansas. Kansas City."

The man nodded, gave him directions across town, then continued on his way. Michael followed the directions and arrived at the Kansas City, Kansas, city hall forty minutes later. After finding his way around, he entered the mayor's office and asked for Mayor Brown. The woman behind the desk gave him a bewildered look and corrected him, saying the mayor's name was James Porter. Michael looked down at the note in his notepad and shook his head.

"No, I'm sorry, but you're wrong. His name is Darius Brown?"

"No, sorry, sir, but you're wrong. The mayor of Kansas City in Kansas is James Porter."

Michael frowned, utterly confused. "Hmmm, I'm sure I was told his name was Brown." He held up the notepad and showed her.

She laughed. "I'm sorry, but you're in the wrong state. You're looking for the mayor of Kansas City, Missouri. You're in Kansas City, Kansas. Both states claim Kansas City."

His bewilderment made her laugh. She turned around and called to another woman in the office.

"Nan? What's the name of the mayor in Missouri?"

"Brown," Nan called back.

She turned back to Michael, still chuckling.

"The good news is, you're only a few minutes away."

She gave Michael directions, and he headed back to where he had searched for the Missouri city hall two blocks from his original location. A trip that should have taken five minutes became two hours.

Michael walks through the lobby and finds a door with the *Mayor's Office* stenciled on the outside in bold letters. After entering, he's greeted by a man seated behind a desk.

"Can I help you, sir?"

"Yes, I'd like to talk with Mayor Brown, please."

"Can I tell him your name? Is he expecting you?"

"My name is Michael Delaney. He's not expecting me, but I must see him."

"And what is this about?"

"Sheriff Winstanley suggested I come. It's regarding Earnest Johns."

The man nods and walks across the room. He knocks, then enters a door in the back before returning a minute later.

"The mayor will see you, but it'll be a few minutes. You can sit there."

He points at a chair along the wall and Michael sits.

After twenty minutes, a man who looks as wide as he is tall exits the door in the back and comes forward, speaking to the man behind the desk.

"Is this him, Harold?" he asks, pointing to Michael.

Harold nods, and Michael wonders why the question was necessary. Nobody else had entered the room since he'd arrived.

The mayor is short, with a sizeable belly and broad shoulders. He wears a white shirt, rolled up to the elbows, a tie, and brown suspenders. A pile of hair extending from the right side of his head covers his balding crown. Michael wonders who he thinks he's fooling with a hairdo like that.

"Mayor Brown," he says, extending his hand.

Michael takes it, impressed by the grip. Although the fingers are short, and the hand is small in the classical sense, the palm is sturdy and muscular.

"Pleased to meet you, Mr. Mayor. Sheriff Winstanley suggested I come to talk with you."

"Oh?"

"Yes, about a man going by the name of Earnest Johns."

The mayor pauses at the name and looks more closely at Michael. "Join me in my office."

After entering, the mayor shuts the door and offers Michael a seat at the desk. He walks around to the other side and sits.

"I don't recognize you. Are you from here?"

Michael shakes his head. "Denver."

"Colorado?"

"Yes."

"What brings you here?"

"Earnest Johns."

"What about him?"

"He matches the description of someone I've been looking for."

"Oh?"

"It's not definite, but I'm pretty sure. Johns matches the description perfectly."

"What did he do?"

"Killed his wife."

The mayor leans back in his chair and whistles. "His name isn't really Earnest Johns, you know. It's Richard Amhurst."

"Are you sure?"

The mayor laughs and slaps his desk, making Michael jump. He leans back in his chair and looks up at the ceiling. "No. That's just it. Do we know *anything* about him?"

After regaining himself, Michael smiles. "I understand someone visited you from Austin, Texas. Told you his name was Richard Amhurst. Amhurst owed him money."

"That's right. Johns was looking for a loan. He wanted to build a nice new hotel here. I loved the idea. Kansas City needs better accommodations. Places we can be proud of. I was introduced to him, and he impressed me. He was very charismatic. I started helping him. I'm just glad Mr. Fredricks came when he did."

"That's the man from Austin? Fredricks?"

"Yes, Carl Fredricks. Nice man. Too bad what Johns did to him."

"What did he do?"

"Stole thousands of dollars from him. Johns, or I should say, Amhurst, was claiming to be an employee of a man by the name of Charles Watson of Houston, Texas. Amhurst got Fredricks to loan Charles Watson money to build a hotel in Austin. Before the hotel was completed, Amhurst left town with the money and piles of debt to unpaid contractors and laborers."

"How were you sure it was Johns?"

"Fredricks had a picture. We also had a handwriting expert analyze his writing and compared it with documents Fredricks showed us. Johns is Amhurst, all right. There's no doubt." The mayor leans forward in his chair, scrutinizing Michael. "Wait a second. You said you're from Denver, Colorado."

"Right."

"And you say he killed his wife there?"

"It looks that way."

"I think you're wasting your time."

"How's that?"

"Johns told me he's from someplace in Illinois. Chicago, maybe. I'm aware of no link in Denver."

"I think he was in Denver before Austin."

The mayor leans back and tugs on his lip. "Maybe."

"Do you have the address of Fredricks in Austin?"

"Are you going there?"

"I think I have to."

Chapter 12

Louise

After boarding the train, Barbara organized our train compartment, and this time, I helped. I loved New York City and all it offered, but I was eager to be back on the train. It was a wild two weeks. I loved the energy the city provided, the sheer mass of numbers. I lived in the second largest city in the United States, but Chicago was only half the size of New York City. The funeral was heartbreaking. My aunt and uncle were in the prime of their lives. It didn't seem real. The *Titanic* was described as a "wonder ship" and "unsinkable." The sinking sent shockwaves through the city and those who knew them. Hundreds of people attended the services, and I learned how highly regarded they were. My aunt was my mother's older sister. She was the mother of six surviving children, all grown adults. My uncle was a successful financier and had left behind a sizeable estate. Father was designated executor of the will and had business to attend to in those duties. Barbara and I spent time with our extended family, but we also had ample time to shop and tour the city.

"Are you ready?" Barbara asked me.

"Just a minute?"

I sat before the mirror in our cramped sleeping compartment, fussing with my hair. It wasn't working, and although I knew I wouldn't be looking my best, I really didn't want to be looking my worst. I was expecting to see Charles at dinner. He'd been scarce since the first day in New York, and I missed him. I couldn't help the excitement I felt at the prospect of being near him again. The initial train ride was everything I had dreamed it could be. Okay, I never would have thought I would sleep with him. The thought had never crossed my mind until it happened. The morning after, I found it difficult to make eye contact with each member of my family. What would my mother say if she knew? My father? Barbara? I knew it was wrong, but I couldn't help myself. I stayed in his bed as long as I dared, listening to him breathe. I didn't wake him when I left, sneaking back into the room with Barbara before she woke. The next day, when I saw him, he acted like nothing had ever happened, and I wondered if I had dreamed it. But then, that afternoon, I found a note tucked in my bag. He told me he longed for me and wanted me to come again that night.

The first night I was nervous. Never had I been kissed before. When I entered his room, he took control, and I let him. I enjoyed it but had a difficult time relaxing. I was too much in my own head. Too unsure. The second night was nothing short of glorious. I felt a closeness to him I could never have imagined. When I left his room, I did so with a longing that had only grown over the last week. I yearned to be with him, and now, back on the train, I knew I'd have my chance.

"Okay," I said to Barbara, "let's go."

We exited the compartment and crossed the train to the dining car. An attendant greeted us and showed us to our table. Our parents were already seated, but Charles was missing. The server greeted us and offered us menus. I was dying to ask after Charles but refrained. I looked at Barbara and wondered if she was thinking the same thing as me, then had another thought. What if she knew something I didn't? My question was answered when she lowered her menu and spoke to my father.

"Is Charles joining us?"

Father held his beer glass in one hand and shook his head. "No, he's staying on in New York for a time."

The disappointment was crushing, but I hid behind my menu, not looking up, afraid my feelings would betray me.

"He met some great contacts who will help him with his hotel."

I could feel tears brimming my eyelids. I had to leave. I needed distance. I stood and placed the menu on the table, keeping my gaze down and away.

"I'm not feeling well."

I stumbled away from the table, nearly knocking over a server. I considered going for our compartment but had started in the wrong direction and couldn't pass the table again. The next best option was the powder room, and I fought the temptation to run. Thankfully, it was vacant, and I went in, locking the door behind me. I sat down on the toilet, pressed a tissue to my face, and cried.

Moments later, a knock came at the door.

"Louise? Honey, are you okay?" My mother asked through the door.

I stifled a sob and shook my head. "No, something isn't right."

I wasn't lying. What Charles had done by not telling me wasn't right, but that's not what I was referring to. The last couple of days I had been off. My stomach felt like it was constantly rolling, especially in the mornings. I was more sensitive to smell. The sight of certain foods was enough to make me vomit.

She knocked again. "Let me in."

I didn't want to see her. But I knew I didn't have a choice. She wasn't giving up, and I needed to face it. I unlocked the door, and she stood there, her gaze penetrating. She couldn't enter. The room was too cramped, dressed as we were.

"Is it your stomach again?"

"Yes," I managed and leaned over. "I'll be okay. I just need to lie down."

I straightened, and she supported me as I walked. We headed through the dining car, past Barbara and Father. I heard Barbara ask after me, but Mother waved her away and said I'd be fine. At last, we reached my sleeping compartment, and I flopped down on the bed, turning away from her into the wall. She sat on the bed and placed a hand on my back.

"Louise?"

I didn't respond.

"I want you to eat better. This obsession with sweet foods has to stop."

It's not what I was eating, but I couldn't tell her that. It was just like her to think she knew everything. To believe only she could determine what was best for me.

My anger flashed, and I nearly lashed out, but I knew she wouldn't go away if I did. Just like answering her questions, the shortest path was to agree. I turned to her and nodded. She's watched me closely, and something about her look made me wonder. Did she know about my feelings for Charles? Did she know what I had done with him? My heart raced under her watchful stare, but I fought it, telling myself to remain calm.

Finally, she stood and moved toward the door.

"I'll come check on you again in a few minutes."

She closed the door, and I was alone. I laid on my back and looked up at the bunk bed above. Tears flowed from my eyes. How could he do this? Didn't he want to see me? Didn't he care for me like I did for him?

I knew his business was important. It was the reason he came. But didn't I matter? I had craved him all week since the last time we'd been together. Didn't he feel the same for me? I laid on my back, covering my pillow in tears, considering the implications, when another thought came to me. *What if he never comes back to Chicago? What if I never see him again?*

Chapter 13

Louise

Three weeks had gone by, and I had heard nothing from Charles. At least, he hadn't contacted me. After arriving home from New York, I expected his return. I imagined Father coming home from the office with Charles at his side. He'd find an opportunity to talk to me or slip me a note and explain where he had been. But it never happened. I asked Barbara if she knew anything, and she didn't. I could tell she was disappointed, but her disappointment was nothing like mine.

After waiting several more days, I summoned the courage to ask Father. We were seated at the dinner table when I asked when we would see Charles again. He glanced up from his plate and looked at me, then Mother, then Barbara. He speared a piece of chicken with his fork and leaned back in his chair.

"I'm not sure if we'll see Charles again."

I heard a sharp intake of breath from Barbara, but my eyes never left Father's. He looked up at the ceiling, talking to no one in particular.

"Last week, I received a letter from him. He thanked me for the connections I helped him make in New York City. He got the financing he was seeking and returned to Texas. He said he hoped to visit again, maybe next year." He leaned forward, looking at Barbara. "I'm sorry."

"Well," Mother said, "I hope business goes well for him."

I could see this wasn't news to her. She had processed the information before. Barbara and I shared a look, and there were tears in her eyes.

Later that night, I asked Barbara how she felt. She told me she was disappointed but didn't know him well and wasn't expecting too much. Nobody ever asked me how I felt. Why would they? How could they know the heartbreak I was feeling? I went to bed feeling like my world had exploded. Like I had nothing left.

The next morning, after vomiting in the toilet, I stared at my reflection in the mirror, knowing what I had to do.

Two hours later, I sat in the park, watching my best friend Emma walk toward me. I stood and hugged her as she joined me on the bench. Emma and I had been friends since we were twelve. She knew me as well as anyone.

"How are you feeling?" she asked.

"The same."

"Does your mom know?"

I said nothing. I didn't have to.

"Louise, you have to tell her."

I shook my head.

"Why?"

"You don't know her like I do."

She looked away and sighed. We sat watching and listening to the birds as they flew from tree to tree. A group of boys played baseball on the field. It was two hours before noon, and the sun was rising quickly. It was going to be a warm day.

"What are you going to do?" she asked.

I looked her in the eye before answering. "I'm going to find him, wherever he is."

"How?"

I looked away. I had been asking myself the same thing.

Chapter 14

Michael

Michael walks into the small consultation room in the jail's front and nods to the jailer.

"Thank you. We'll be fine."

Frank, the jailer, a burly fellow with a long, straggly beard and wavy, light-brown hair, looks at him, then at the prisoner before nodding. He steps around Michael and closes the door.

Michael and the prisoner stare at each other. Michael sits in the old wooden chair opposite him. The prisoner rests his hands on the table, his wrists shackled, his face void of emotion, just like before.

"I just came from Mayor Brown's office. You know him, right? We had an interesting discussion. I learned a bit more about you." Michael watches him for some type of reaction. There isn't one. "The only problem was, we couldn't agree on what to call you. The mayor preferred Ernest Johns, while I liked Richard Amhurst. Which name is your favorite?"

For the first time, a slight smile appears on his lips.

"Of course, I don't think either of those names are real. I think your name is Thomas Slater, and you're from Colorado Springs. Do you mind if I call you Tommy?"

Rather than grow angry at Michael's flippant attitude, the smile grows broader. The blue eyes dance with amusement. He leans back and folds his hands, but he still says nothing.

"Oh, come on? It's just us. They've got you dead to rights on the fraud charges. They know you went by different names. What does talking to me hurt?"

No response.

"Do you like Texas?"

The question catches him off guard, and the prisoner frowns.

"I've never been. I'm planning to go. I'm going to talk with this Carl Fredricks fella. The mayor recommended it. Said he might be able to help me. The thing is, I really don't want to go. I didn't really love coming here. Texas is even farther from home. I'm a Rocky Mountains guy. You get me too far away from the mountains and my happiness drops. You know what I mean?"

The prisoner still says nothing.

Michael leans back in his chair and looks at the ceiling. "Come on, Johns or Amhurst or whatever you want to be called. Save me the trip. Have you ever been to Denver? Colorado Springs? Does the name Helen Covington mean anything to you? Maybe Helen Slater?"

Michael watches his eyes, hoping to see the pupils dilate. Nothing.

"You're going to make me go to Texas, aren't you?"

Michael leans forward in his chair and grabs the armrests, preparing to push himself up, but stops. His face inches from the prisoner. When he speaks, it's in a whisper.

"What other bodies am I going to find there? What other women did you kill?"

The prisoner smiles a smug smile. It's everything Michael can do not to pull out his gun and shoot him in the head. He would too, except he's still not sure this is the man he's looking for. It might be he's simply a fraudster. Maybe he's killed no one. It's that doubt that keeps Michael from exacting the revenge he so desperately craves.

Michael straightens, looks down at him, then walks to the door. Before he exits, he stops and speaks without turning around. "I did learn one very interesting nugget from the mayor. He said you were married in Austin. You and your wife had a child. A boy. I wonder where they are now. Maybe I can find them."

Chapter 15

Louise

After dinner, Barbara and I went on a walk. I considered telling her what I was planning, but knew she'd never be able to keep the secret and abandoned the idea. Maybe she'd even try to talk me out of it. When we returned home, as was our custom, we all separated into the corners of the house. Father to his study, Mother to her craft room, Barbara and I to our bedrooms. Most days, I wouldn't see them again until the next morning; however, knowing tonight would be my last, I wished them all a good night before bed. I went to Barbara first. She was sketching in a notebook and seemed annoyed by the interruption. Father was next. He was sipping whiskey and poring over some business papers. He barely looked up as I wished him a pleasant sleep. Finally, I went to Mother. She was reading in her craft room. I never understood how she could read while swaying back and forth in her rocking chair. The motion would make me sick. She eyed me suspiciously as I said good night, and I thought she might ask me what was going on, but she didn't. Instead, she responded with a good night of her own, and I walked out. I could feel her eyes on me as I left.

Last was Nibbles. When I went into his room, he sat on his perch looking out the window. The sun hadn't set yet, but the room was engulfed in shadow. He looked at me and squawked. I extended my finger to him, and he climbed on, turning so he could face me. It was silly, but in a way, he was the most difficult to say goodbye to. I could be honest with him. I held him on my finger, talking to him about my plans. He would move and sway, occasionally squawking. After a few minutes, I put him in his cage and covered it.

For the next three hours, I lay in bed, waiting. I ran over my plans again and again, anticipating every possible scenario. Finally, at two a.m., I rose from my bed and changed my clothes. After leaving the park, Emma and I had gone around town gathering my wardrobe. At the secondhand store, I bought an old sundress, an old pair of shoes with no heel, and a blond wig. I stuffed my long, dark hair under the wig, then placed a sunbonnet over the top. I checked myself in the mirror, happy to see how different I looked. Grabbing the prepacked luggage piece I had taken to New York City, I crept to the door, aware of any slight creak in the flooring.

The hallway was quiet and dark. Holding my bag against my chest, I walked down the hall and reached the staircase. I took extra care, wincing at any groan in the wood. When I finally reached the bottom, I entered Father's study and went to the small safe behind his liquor cabinet. It was difficult to see with so little light, but I felt my way along the wall, stubbing my toe on a chair in the process. I held my breath and tugged on the door, praying I wouldn't need to resort to my backup plan. Thankfully, it opened. I'd always wondered why my father had a safe. Never had I seen it locked. I always thought it would make more sense to hide his money somewhere else if he didn't bother locking it. As I opened the door and reached inside, a wave of guilt rolled over me, and I considered leaving the money, but I knew I couldn't. Without the money, I couldn't make it out of Chicago.

I removed one hundred dollars and stuffed the money into the bottom of my bag. I walked out of the study, through the kitchen, and to the back door. As I opened the door, I heard a sound behind me. I turned, expecting to see Mother, but saw nothing. I stood still, looking back, listening in the dark. After a minute, I was satisfied I was alone and stepped out of the house. I softly closed the door, walked around the house to the street, and began my three-mile journey to the train station.

As I walked, I took several deep breaths, knowing I had crossed my first test but also that the most difficult was still to come. I had to find Charles, but where and how? When my father had introduced us in the theater, he had said, "Charles

Watson of Houston, Texas." Having no reason to doubt, I believed that was his home. But when I had met Charles in the park, he told me he had only asked to court Barbara because that's what my father wanted. It made me wonder how much of anything he told me was true. Then, when I was with him in his private compartment on the train, I noticed a train ticket on his bedstand. It was old and wrinkled, but I could clearly see it was a ticket from Austin, Texas, to Kansas City. I knew he had to be in one of those three cities. I just didn't know which.

As I walked, I noticed how different my hometown was at night. I'd never been out this late. The streets were deserted, and other than an occasional dog barking, silent. Chicago had been my home since birth. Other than my freshman year at South Bend, it was all I knew. Whenever I traveled, it was with my parents. I could never remember feeling alone, and now I was. I was headed to a city I didn't know, looking for a man I barely knew, and carrying his baby. I was running away from the mistakes I had made and the consequences that would follow.

When I reached the train station, the night sky had given way to the first signs of sunrise. Shadows had appeared, and the clear sky above morphed from black to blue. I walked into the station and looked around, hoping to find someone who could direct me. A large train sat on the rails, and people occupied benches all around. Most looked dirty and hungry. Many stretched across the benches, sleeping. I saw a man wearing a uniform and hat, like those that had been on the train to New York.

I approached him and asked, "Sir, where might I buy a ticket?"

He glanced at me with disdain, looking away and pointing to his right.

"Thank you," I told him and walked in the direction he showed.

As I walked, I wondered about his reaction. The attendants on the train from weeks ago were so pleasant and happy to help. This man acted like I was a bother. I looked down and noticed the holes in my clothes and the plain, dirty shoes. I realized I looked similar to all those people lying on the benches in the station. I was like them in his eyes. After several paces, I saw a sign that said, "Ticket Office." I entered, and an attendant stood behind a counter.

"Can I have a train ticket, please?"

"Where?"□

"Pardon?"

He rolls his eyes. "Where are you going?"

"Oh…Austin, Texas, please."

He shakes his head. "No trains are going to Austin. You'll have to connect through Kansas City."

"Oh, okay. That's fine."

"Three dollars."

I reached into my bag and pulled out the stack of money I had stolen from my father. I separated three dollars and handed them to him. He eyed me suspiciously, then handed back a ticket. I gripped the ticket and walked out to the platform. I looked at the clock and saw I had thirty minutes until boarding. I looked around for a seat, but all the benches were taken. Having no other choice, I stood on the platform with my bag at my feet. After fifteen minutes, smoke filled the air. The smell made my stomach roll, and I looked around for a garbage can. I picked up my bag and walked to one, then wretched into it. When I pulled back, the smell from the can made me wretch again. I had no kerchief or tissue and wiped my mouth with the back of my hand. I looked around and saw people forming lines in front of the train doors.

I walked over and got in line. After ten minutes, a man came by and opened the doors. The big man standing behind me pushed forward and caused me to run into the woman standing in front of me. She turned around and glared at me. The smell of body odor filled my nostrils, and my stomach rolled again. I stepped out of line and raced to the garbage, fighting the vomit rising in my throat. I reached it just in time and wretched into the can. I stepped back and took a deep breath, wiping my mouth. When I looked back at the line, it was mostly gone. Only a few people remained. I walked back and stepped up on the stairs. My bag was wide, and I had to fight to squeeze it through the doors.

When I finally reached the top, I was exhausted and panting. I stood in the car's hallway and breathed deeply. An attendant came by, and I called out to him, showing my ticket.

"Sir, where is my compartment?"

He gave me a curious look, then took the ticket from me, examining it. He waved his arm and said, "You're in it." He saw my confusion and explained. "Sorry, Your Majesty, this ticket is for a seat on the train. Any seat. Find one and sit down."

I took my ticket from him and walked into the large room with rows of occupied seats. The noise was deafening with crying babies, loud conversation, and laughter. The smell was a concoction of body odor, cigarette smoke, and alcohol. I scanned the seats and found only one unoccupied. It was between two large men. I walked to the row and tapped the nearest man on the shoulder.

"Can I sit there?"

He looked at me, then stood and allowed me past. I sat in the seat, and he returned to his, squishing into me. The man to my right glanced away from the window, looked me up and down, then looked back out the window.

There I sat, between two large, strange men. All my possessions were on my lap. It was smelly, loud, crowded. Staring at the seat in front of me, tears filled my eyes.

Chapter 16

Louise

I felt the shudder of brakes and looked out the window, expecting to see a city. Instead, I saw nothing. Beyond the train tracks, it looked as if man didn't exist. Maybe ever. There were no buildings, telephone poles, or roads. I stood and leaned my head out the window to get a better look. In front of the train, in the distance, I saw a shack. Beyond it, nothing but fields and trees. I looked at my watch. According to the train schedule, we should have been arriving in Austin. I wondered if something was wrong. Maybe we were making an unscheduled stop.

A minute later, the train attendant came down the aisle, announcing, "Taylor Station, Austin, Texas."

I looked back outside. *Where?*

The train came to a stop, and I carried my bag past several passengers, squeezing it down the aisle. The attendant stood by the door.

"This is Austin?" I asked.

"No, this is Taylor. Austin is thirty miles away."

"Oh, so should I stay on?"

"For Austin?"

"Yes."

"Not on this train. This is the closest you'll get to Austin. The next stop is Houston."

I opened my mouth to ask another question, but he cut me off by pointing to the two people behind me, then asked, "Are you getting off?"

I sighed and left the train. I cleared the bottom of the steps and set down my bag, wondering how this was even a station. It was one small building that looked like a toolshed. I looked around for some symbol of civilization but didn't see any.

The two men who were behind me had cleared the station, and the whistle sounded on the train. I considered jumping back on board but decided there was little point. I picked up my bag and walked to the entrance of the "station" as the train pulled out.

A man stood leaning on the building, an enormous hat on his head. He was of average height, with a lean build and a dark mustache that curled at the ends, a pipe sticking out of the corner of his mouth. He was a handsome man, but quite a few years older than me. Probably in his forties.

He looked at me and tipped his hat. "Ma'am."

Although I was still wearing old clothing, I looked more like myself. In Kansas City, I got rid of my blond wig and cleaned myself up. I searched the town for Charles but found no leads and came down here to Austin.

"Is this Austin?"

"Nope. Austin's that way."

He turned and pointed in a direction that I assumed was south.

"How far?"

"Half day's ride."

I turned and looked toward the point as he puffed on his pipe. I wasn't sure what I was looking for. Some sign of civilization, I guess.

"How would one get to Austin from here?"

He removed the pipe from the side of his mouth and smiled. "Arrange for transportation before you come."

I nodded. "And what if you didn't? What alternatives might someone have?"

He shook his head. "I'm afraid I don't know what to tell you."

Panic rose in my chest. He looked at me and took a drag on his pipe. "Where in Austin?"

"I'm looking for the Thorn Hotel."

He shook his head. "Haven't heard of it."

"It's on Brazos Street?" I said, hoping there was such a street in the town. There wasn't one in Kansas City.

He chewed on his lip. "I know Brazos. Right downtown. Don't know the hotel, though."

His reply filled me with excitement. Not only was there a Brazos Street but there was a downtown.

He looked around and puffed on his pipe, blowing out smoke. "You have money?"

"Some."

He sighed. "Been thinkin' 'bout goin' to Austin. Got some business there." He looked me up and down. "You know how to ride?"

"A horse?"

"No, an airplane. Yes...a horse."

I shook my head.

He blew out a lungful of air. "I could take my buggy. But it's going to cost you."

"How much?"

"Ten dollars."

If someone had said a month before, I would have been standing in the middle of Texas eager to jump in a buggy with a man I had never met. I'd have laughed until my sides hurt. Instead, I smiled and agreed.

"It's going to be a few minutes. You'll have to wait here," he said and walked away. He climbed on his horse and left.

I picked up my bag and walked under what little shade the small building offered. As I watched him ride away, I worried he might not come back. Within seconds, I could no longer see him. I surveyed the area and saw what I already knew—I was completely alone. It was late morning, and the sun was blistering hot. Summers in Chicago could get warm, but nothing like this. I looked around, seeing lots of trees, and wondered how they could survive in such heat.

As I stood, baking in air that felt like the inside of an oven, my thirst grew. When I was a little girl, my mother used to tell me to suck on my tongue when I was thirsty and she had nothing to give me. I hadn't tried it in several years, but now I was desperate. I stood, trying to suck my tongue, hopelessly searching for relief.

After thirty minutes, I saw a small horse and buggy coming my way in the distance. When it reached me, the man jumped down and grabbed my bag.

"Sorry about the wait. It took longer than expected."

"It's fine," I said, grateful he came back.

I climbed up into the buggy. He sat next to me and handed me a canteen.

"Water?"

I thanked him and took it as he whipped the reins and we jostled down the dirt path. The water was warm, but I didn't care. It tasted like the most delicious thing that had ever touched my lips. After drinking half the bottle, I put the cap back on and handed it to him.

"Where you from?"

I hesitated before answering. "Kansas City."

"Nope," he said, eyeing me.

"Yes."

"Nope," he said, smiling.

I turned away, looking out across the never-ending fields of green and brown.

"Chicago or New York?"

I turned back to him. "What?"

"You're a city girl, clear as the mustache on my face. So, which city? New York or Chicago?"

I looked down. "Chicago."

He nodded and snapped the reins. "What ya fixin' to do round here?"

"I'm trying to find someone."

He stared at me, then turned his attention back to the path.

"Do you know many people in Austin?" I asked.

"Some."

"Do you know a Charles Watson?"

"Nope."

The conversation stopped, and for a long time, we said nothing, bumping along the path that eventually became more dirt and less brush.

"How old are ya?" he asked.

I looked at him, but he didn't look at me. I couldn't believe he would ask that. It wasn't proper, even if he was my elder. I ignored it, but he wouldn't let me.

"Nineteen? Twenty?"

I didn't respond. He was close, just a year too much.

"This Watson feller, you love him?"

I said nothing.

He nodded. "I'll get ya to Austin, and I won't even charge ya. The only thing you'll have to pay me is a moment's attention." He stared into my eyes. "You hear me?"

I nodded.

"You go find this Watson feller, say what ya been fixin' to say, then come back here and get back on the train. Go back to Chicago. Back where you belong. Understand me?"

I stared at him, unbelieving that a stranger would talk to me like this. It unnerved me, but he wouldn't look away. He just kept staring. Finally, I nodded.

Chapter 17

Louise

I'd never been so eager to see a building. After riding in the buggy with Gerald for miles that seemed to never end, civilization emerged from the dusty trail. Austin was a town compared to Chicago, but at least it was a town. As we approached downtown, the dusty trail gave way to packed dirt roads and buildings. At first, the buildings were residential, but as we neared the city center, they gave way to multiple-story buildings of business. In the distance, I could see a large, brown, domed structure, and I asked Gerald about it.

"That's the Texas State Capitol Building."

"Austin is the state capital?"

"Yes, ma'am. That building is taller than the country capitol in DC." He looked at me and smiled. "If you haven't noticed, we Texans like everything big. Just look at my hat." For the first time since leaving Chicago, I felt myself smile. "Now, where am I dropping you?"

I'd had plenty of time to think about that and was ready with the answer. "I need a hotel downtown. Something near Brazos."

Gerald rubbed his stubbly chin and rattled off three names. Only one stood out, The Driskill, and I asked him to take me there.

Five minutes later, he stopped the buggy in front of a large four-story building, climbed down, and offered me his hand. After retrieving my luggage, he tipped his hat, climbed aboard, and snapped the reins. I turned and looked at the extensive building and entered. The sparkling white marble floors and columns impressed me. Chandeliers adorned the ceiling throughout the lobby, and a large *D* painted onto the tile in the center reminded visitors of the hotel's name.

Although the hotel was nothing grander than what I'd seen in Chicago or New York, I felt painfully underdressed and self-conscious. Knowing I had no other choice, I approached the main desk. A man in a hotel uniform watched me approach.

"Yes, ma'am. How may I be of help?"

"I'd like a room, please."

He eyed me carefully. "Our room rates start at two dollars per night."

"That'll be fine," I said.

"Very good. How many nights do you intend to stay with us?"

"At least three. I'm not sure just yet."

"Very good. I'll need the payment upfront. Will that be a problem?"

I shook my head and handed him the six dollars. After asking for my name and having me sign the guest list, he offered me the key and asked a bellhop to assist me to my room. When I closed the door, exhaustion overtook me, and I collapsed onto the bed.

I didn't wake up again until the next morning. After bathing and changing into the best dress I had, I looked in the mirror and saw my old self. A grin crossed my lips. If all went well, I'd see Charles that day.

I continued getting ready, fixing my hair, applying makeup, and spritzing some perfume before heading to the lobby. I was starving, having not eaten since the train yesterday morning. The lobby of the hotel had a dining room, and I requested a table.

After a large breakfast of eggs, bacon, and orange juice, I paid my bill and exited. When I reached the front desk, I saw the same man who had helped me yesterday.

"Sir, I have a question."

He looked at me, and I could tell he didn't recognize me, trying to place how he might know me.

"I'm a guest of the hotel, staying in Room 307."

Surprise registered on his face, and I could see he was flustered. "I'm sorry, miss. I didn't recognize you. How can I be of help?"

He was nice enough yesterday, but there was a difference today. His eyes twinkled, and his smile was broad.

"Are you familiar with the Thorn Hotel?"

"I am. You aren't planning on leaving us, are you?"

"No, a friend owns the hotel, and I'd like to pay a visit."

"You're in luck. The hotel is only a quarter of a mile from here. You can walk along Sixth Street two blocks, and it will be on your left."

He took out a map of the downtown and pointed to our current location and Charles's hotel. I thanked him and headed out the doors.

As I started down Sixth Street, I looked up at the sun. It wasn't over ten in the morning, and already the sun was blazing. I could only imagine what temperature it would reach in the afternoon. As I walked along, I took notice of my surroundings. A man herded a team of cattle down the middle of the street. Things differed from Chicago, even the cows. They had large, long horns that extended from the middle of their foreheads. They looked dangerous, and I couldn't believe how confident the man seemed in guiding them down the street. I wondered what would happen if you were gored by one. Would it kill you?

After they passed, I found there weren't many people on the street other than me, and those who were made me feel overdressed. The women wore simple sundresses, while the men wore trousers and light cotton shirts. The men wore immense hats, and the women covered their heads with bonnets. It made sense. Headwear provided some relief from the sun. I nodded to several as I continued along, and they smiled, nodding back.

When I reached the corner of Sixth and Lavaca, I saw the hotel. On the outside, it looked complete. It wasn't as large as the Driskill, but it was new, and the outside featured a balcony that wrapped around the exterior. I saw laborers carrying tools and other supplies inside through the front door. I hesitated, then took a deep breath and crossed the street.

After reaching the front doors, I ducked inside, following a couple of men carrying pails of paint. One man turned around and stopped me.

"Miss, the hotel isn't open."

"I understand. I'm looking for Mr. Charles Watson."

"Mr. Watson's not here. Only his manager, Mr. Amhurst."

My disappointment must have shown on my face because he rushed to explain.

"I've never seen Mr. Watson. He's never been here when I've been here. I'm sorry."

I thanked him and turned to go but stopped, turning back around. "Can I see the manager?"

"Mr. Amhurst?"

"Yes."

"Certainly. I'll see if he's free."

He asked me to wait, and he and the other man left, heading down the hall. The lobby of this hotel wasn't grand, but it was modern and nice. It had none of the grand columns of the Driskill. But the windows were large and allowed plenty of light. The floor was freshly laid wood, and I could still smell the lacquer they had used. After a couple of minutes, I saw a man coming down the hallway toward me. He was tall and lean. Although not wearing a suit, like in Chicago, I would have recognized him anywhere. The natural light from the windows was to my back, and I could see he was squinting, trying to see who I was. When he was only a few feet away, I saw the surprise in his eyes.

"Louise?"

"Hello, Charles."

He looked around, then grabbed me by the elbow and walked me toward the windows.

"What are you doing here? Did your father bring you?" he whispered.

I shook my head. "I came alone."

I thought he'd be pleased to see me. But he wasn't. I got the impression he was ashamed to have me there.

"Where did you come from? Why?"

"To see you. What do you mean?"

He looked at me, his lips tight. Behind him, a man approached. It was the same one who had stopped me earlier.

"Sorry to interrupt. Mr. Amhurst, we have a question."

Charles turned to look at him. *Amhurst?*

"Give me just a minute. I'll be right with you," he told him and waved him away. Once he was out of earshot, he turned back to me. "Louise, you shouldn't have come. I can't see you right now."

His words pierced my heart.

"Charles, I need to talk to you. I've come all this way."

He held up his hand, and for a second, I thought he was going to strike me. Instead, he smoothed back his hair, leaning forward. His voice was a whisper.

"I can't do this right now. Are you staying somewhere in town?"

"The Driskill Hotel."

"Tomorrow I can come. We can talk then."

He turned to leave, but I reached out and grabbed his hand.

"Tonight."

He shook his head, pulling his hand away. His whisper turned to a hiss. "No, I have a banquet tonight in the capitol. Tomorrow."

Without another word, he spun and stalked away.

Chapter 18

Louise

After leaving Charles at his hotel, I went back to mine. I hid my face as I walked past people on Sixth Street. Tears streamed down my face, but I couldn't let them see. I didn't want questions. I didn't want offers for help. After reaching the Driskill, I took the stairs back to my room. Once inside, I collapsed onto the bed and kicked and screamed. Shock and anger overwhelmed me.

Eventually, I turned over and stared at the ceiling. Anger gave way to heartbreak. I was shattered. Coming all this way, I wasn't sure what to expect. Of course, I dreamed he'd look at me the way he did in Chicago. He'd smile that delicious smile, wrap me in his arms, and kiss me. His joy would be obvious. That's what I had expected. I told myself not to expect that much. He'd be shocked, after all. Maybe he'd be reserved, like he was around my sister and parents. But I never imagined that I'd see what I saw today—disgust in his eyes. In Chicago, when we were alone, he looked at me so provocatively it took my breath away. It was as if he was undressing me with his mind. Today, in that building, he looked at me with anger and resentment. *How? How could this be the same man?*

My emotions ran the gambit, from surprise to hurt to anger to disappointment back to anger again. I had traveled a thousand miles to see him. He told me he would return to Chicago and didn't. I gave myself to him. How dare he toss me aside like a used tissue. I wanted answers, and I wasn't about to wait until tomorrow.

I got up, bathed again, tidied my dress, fixed my hair and makeup, and set off for the capitol building walking along Congress Street. As I reached the exterior garden, I walked along the stone path leading to the front doors. Lovely green pecan trees bracketed the path.

I reached the front entrance, pushed open the big wooden doors, and stepped inside. I didn't know where I was going or what I was going to do when I got there. I just knew I couldn't wait until tomorrow.

The room I entered was empty. Nothing but me and the white columns. I wondered what it was with white columns in this town. I looked around, expecting to see some type of banquet, but saw nothing. I walked through the large, white archway and entered a much larger room. I'd been inside substantial buildings before in Chicago and New York, but the power I felt in this room was palpable. I walked to the center of the room and gazed up, leaning back as I stared at the ceiling. I was standing under the vast dome, visible from everywhere in Austin. In the center was a solitary star. I remembered seeing the same star on the state flag and wondered about its significance.

A cough brought me out of my trance, and I looked around, trying to find the source. An older man, my grandfather's age, stood in the hallway leading away from the rotunda. He was tall and wore a white suit with white boots and a large white hat. A toothpick protruded from the side of his mouth.

"You lost?" he asked.

"I'm looking for someone."

He removed the toothpick from his mouth and walked toward me. "Who's that?"

I realized I wasn't sure of the name to give and fumbled for a response.

"Um...is there a banquet here tonight?"

He picked at his teeth with the toothpick. "Yep. Just down the hall there."

I thanked him and walked toward the hallway.

"Someone I can help you find?"

I pretended I didn't hear him and continued walking. Halfway down the hall, I heard a multitude of voices coming from behind a door. Without thinking, I pushed open the door. The room was full of people. Most held drinks. I was invisible as I walked among them, scanning their faces. Almost immediately, I saw him. He was wearing a dark suit, just like the first time I met him at the theater. But there was one significant difference. His arm was around a tall, lean blond woman. Her hair was beautifully braided, and she wore a long, white, sleek gown. A large pearl necklace adorned her neck, and a matching bracelet hung from her wrist. Their attention was on the large man in front of them.

My blood boiled at the sight, and before I could stop myself, words fell out of my mouth.

"You liar!" I screamed.

The conversation stopped, and I went from being invisible to the focal point of the room. Every eye turned in my direction, including Charles's.

Committed, I walked toward him, pointing at his chest. "You lied to me. You lied about everything."

The blond turned from me to him in confusion. All attention shifted to Charles. He looked at me, paused, then smiled and released the blond. With a curious look on his face, his blue eyes hooded, he walked toward me.

"I'm sorry, dear. There must be some mistake. Let's go talk. Let's get this whole misunderstanding straightened out."

He grabbed me by the wrist and squeezed hard while turning back to the crowd of people. He moved in front of me as I gasped in pain. Like a magician on a stage, he raised his other hand, deflecting the attention from me and his grip.

"My friend from the north isn't well. She's had a long journey and gets confused by the heat. I'll be back. Let me just get her taken care of."

All eyes remained on us as we walked out of the room. He still held my wrist, but his grip wasn't as tight as before. When we cleared the doors, he walked me past a secluded hallway and down a flight of stairs. When we reached the bottom, he looked around and then turned on me. His face was engulfed in shadow, but I could see the tightness of his jaw and the burning in his eyes.

"What do you think you're doing, little girl?" he hissed, keeping his voice low.

I looked at him and wondered who he was. This was not the man I knew in Chicago.

"Do you think I'm going to allow you to come here and ruin everything for me?"

I took a step back, shocked into silence.

"What do you want, Louise?"

I stared at him, realizing I didn't know the answer to that question.

"I'm pregnant."

He stared at me, not comprehending. The cold fury was gone from his voice. "What?"

"I'm pregnant."

He frowned, disbelief in his eyes. "Are you sure?"

"Very."

"When? How?"

"The train... Did you forget?"

He put his hand to his forehead, looking away from me and back up the stairs.

Something about saying it aloud had brought a rush of shame. Now that I'd said it, I could only think of one thing—I wanted to get away from him. I needed distance. I turned to head back up the stairs, but he grabbed me.

"Wait, wait. I'm sorry. I didn't know. You're sure?"

I sighed and pulled away. "Positive."

"When will you have the baby?"

"I'm not sure. Maybe seven months."

He looked at my stomach. "But I can't even tell? You look the same."

"It's still early. But I have to go."

I started climbing the stairs, but he followed me, suddenly contrite.

"Louise, I'm sorry. Let me come to the hotel tomorrow. We need to talk about this."

I shook my head, but even as I did, I knew he was right. We needed to talk.

"Please? I'll come for lunch. Let's just talk."

We had reached the top and were near the banquet hall when I stopped, turned around, and looked up at him.

"Tomorrow," he said, nodding.

"Okay."

Chapter 19

Louise

The next morning, when I came down the stairs for breakfast, I saw Charles seated in the lobby. He looked up from his newspaper, saw me, and smiled. Then he stood and walked toward me. I kept my expression flat, emotionless.

Last night, after coming back from the capitol, I was exhausted. Never in my life had I felt that sort of fatigue. All I could think of was sleep. Mother used to say she was most tired in her first three months of pregnancy. I guess making a baby is hard work. I could barely lift my feet above the floor as I walked down the hall to my room. After undressing and climbing into bed, I had expected to fall asleep. But I didn't. I tossed and turned. So many thoughts plagued my mind. So many questions.

I wondered what I should do. I knew I couldn't go home. I had left to avoid facing the mistakes I had made, and those mistakes were even greater now. I couldn't put my parents through the shame of having a daughter pregnant out of wedlock and kicked out of college for plagiarism. Running away only added to it. Returning would only make things harder.

"Good morning," he said, smiling and looking at his watch. "It's almost a good afternoon. I thought you'd never come down."

"How long have you been here?"

He shrugged. "A couple hours."

"Oh, sorry."

He waved a hand.

"It's fine. It gave me a chance to read the whole newspaper...twice."

He chuckled, but I turned and looked toward the dining room. It seemed they were closing, and my heart leaped. Pregnancy gave me more than a constant feeling of exhaustion; I was always hungry. The hunger pangs I was experiencing were like nothing I had ever felt before. The only problem was, I couldn't always keep the food down.

He saw me looking at the dining room. "Breakfast?"

I nodded, and he took my hand. A man stood at the front of the restaurant.

"We'd like a table by the window, please," Charles said.

The man looked at him, then at me, then back at him.

"I'm afraid we just ended breakfast service, sir. Come back in an hour for lunch."

Charles looked at me, and he must have seen my desperation. He fished in his jacket pocket and held out a two-dollar bill to the man.

"I'd appreciate you making an exception."

The man reluctantly took the money. He walked us to a table along the windows. Once we were seated, he handed us menus, but I didn't take mine.

"Two eggs, toast, and coffee, please," I said.

He looked at Charles, and Charles chuckled.

"I'll take the same."

The man left, and Charles looked at me. We were virtually alone in the dining hall, but I still felt it necessary to whisper.

"Hunger is greater in my condition."

He nodded and smiled. "I can imagine. Eat all you want."

We stared at each other, neither knowing what to say next. Finally, Charles broke the silence.

"Louise...I'm sorry. I've been under an inordinate amount of pressure since returning from New York. The hotel has had delays in opening, and my investors are getting anxious. I wasn't expecting to see you, and I didn't handle it well. But I want you to know that I'm so glad you came. I'm happy you're here."

The server returned with the coffee, and after adding cream and sugar, I sipped some and then put down the cup.

"It didn't seem like you were happy to see me."

Charles extended his hand across the table. It was the most affectionate I'd seen him be in public, and I liked it. But I didn't give him my hand.

"Honey, you just caught me by surprise, is all. I'm excited that you came. I can't believe you're sitting here with me in Austin. It's a dream come true."

His eyes nearly twinkled as he said it. This was the Charles I had known in Chicago. The one I had given myself to on the train to New York.

"Who was that woman?"

"What woman?"

The server returned with our eggs and toast, and our conversation stopped until he walked away.

"The woman you were with last night at the banquet."

"Oh, her? Nobody. The daughter of a politician here. She's just like Barbara. I have no interest in her."

"Then why was your arm around her?" I asked, covering my mouth full of eggs.

He waved his hand. "Honestly, that was nothing. Her father is the building inspector here. If I showed her some interest, he might push my permit through faster, which would get the hotel open and the investors off my back."

I looked at him skeptically, but he just smiled.

"Cross my heart." He mimed an *x* over his heart.

He extended his hand to me again, and I reluctantly gave him mine.

"Why did that man call you Richard Amhurst?"

"What man?"

"The worker in your hotel said you were the manager and your name was Richard Amhurst."

I felt his body tense. Although we'd been speaking in low voices, he leaned closer and whispered, "I've told no one this. You'll be the only person to know." My eyes were glued to his. "I am Richard Amhurst."

"What?"

"Well, I should say, I'm both. I'm Richard Amhurst and I'm Charles Watson." His blue eyes were like Lake Michigan on a cloudless summer day. "Richard Amhurst is my real name. I made up Charles Watson. I created him."

"What? How? Why?"

He looked down at his watch, then back up at me.

"I'm sorry, Louise. I have to go. I've got a very important meeting at my hotel."

"Charles," I said as he stood.

He hadn't released my hand and leaned forward to kiss it. "Let's go to dinner tonight. I'll explain everything."

Chapter 20

Michael

Michael looks down at his notepad, then back up at the building. The name on the building matches the name in his notes. He crosses Sixth Street and enters through the large glass doors. A vast desk sits in the lobby, with a man standing behind it.

"Welcome to the Thorn Hotel. Checking in?"

"How much for a night?"

"Single or double?"

"Single."

"One dollar and fifty cents."

Michael fishes around in his pocket and pulls out what money he has. He knows he's got to make it stretch.

"How 'bout a buck?"

The man shakes his head. "Sorry, sir. That's a reduced rate already. It's less than we charged a year ago."

"A year ago, huh? You've been here that long?"

"I've been here since we opened."

"You have?" Michael slaps a dollar fifty on the table. "I'll take that room."

The man grins. "Very good, sir. I'll need some information from you for the registry. Your name, please?"

"Michael Delaney."

"And where do you hail from?"

"Denver."

"Oh, I'd love to see the mountains of Denver. I've heard so much about them."

"They are pretty spectacular."

The clerk lays the registry on the desk and hands Michael a pen. "Sign, please."

Michael takes the pen and signs his name.

The clerk turns around and pulls a key from the board of keys and numbers behind him, then turns back to Michael.

"Room 207. Just up the stairs and to your right."

Michael picks up his bag, takes the key from him, then turns toward the stairs, but stops as if he's just thought of something.

"Does Charles Watson still own this hotel?"

The clerk frowns and looks skeptically back at Michael. "Why do you ask?"

Michael turns back and stands beside the desk. "I heard maybe he doesn't. That he might have been involved in something."

The man eyes Michael, then walks to the side of the desk and looks down the hall behind him before returning. "What did you hear?"

Michael shakes his head and shrugs. "Oh, not much. Just that maybe he skipped town owing people a lot of money."

The clerk leans forward and drops his voice. "There was no Charles Watson."

"Come again?"

"He never existed."

"Then who owned the hotel?"

"Richard Amhurst. He made up a man named Charles Watson. I don't know all the specifics, but he got loans and made Mr. Fredricks cosign on them. He skipped town, and Mr. Fredricks was left with all the debt."

"Wow!"

"Yeah," the clerk says, nodding.

"So, Mr. Fredricks owns the hotel?"

"Now he does." The clerk leans his head to the side. "Come to think of it, he always has, I guess. He's a good man. Shame what Amhurst did to him."

Michael nods. "Where could I find Mr. Fredricks?"

"He comes here every night around six to check on the lodgings and collect any money received. But I don't want any trouble for Mr. Fredricks. He's a good man. He's already been through a lot."

Michael shakes his head. "Oh, I don't mean any trouble. I just want to ask him a few questions. I think I can help him."

Chapter 21

Louise

Charles was waiting for me in the lobby at six p.m. when I came downstairs. He wore a black suit with a red tie. His crisp white shirt was shown through the front of the jacket. He stood smiling, leaning against a wall. I thought he might kiss me when he approached, but he took me by the hand and led me out the door.

"Where are we going?" I asked.

"Does it matter?" he said. It seemed like such an odd response. Did everything have to be a mystery?

"I guess not."

We walked three blocks, then crossed the road and entered a brick building with a sign over the front door that read, *Scholz Garten*. A man in a white shirt and suspenders greeted us as we entered. When he spoke, I noticed an unusual accent. His *w*'s sounded like *v*'s.

"Welcome to Scholz Garten. Two tonight?"

Charles nodded, and the man walked us through the restaurant to a table near the back against the wall. There were several other tables spread throughout the room, but most were empty.

"Fine?" he asked.

"Great!" Charles said.

The man pulled out a chair for me. Charles took off his jacket and draped it over the back of the chair. When we were seated, our host handed us menus.

"I be back," he said and walked away.

"What is this place?" I asked, looking around.

"A restaurant," he said, chuckling.

"I know but..."

"Have you ever had German food before?"

"I don't think so. What's it like?"

"I love it. How can you go wrong? Breaded meats, sausage, noodles, potatoes, sauerkraut."

"Sauer-what?"

"Sauerkraut. It's cabbage that they ferment. It's got a sour taste to it. Hence the name. Kind of like a pickle, but different. Do you like pickles?"

I scrunched up my face. "Not really."

"Oh...well, maybe don't order it then. I'll let you taste mine."

The man with the long, gray beard returned. "What you have?" he asked, holding a pencil and a notepad.

"Two beers, one each, and I'll have a bratwurst with spaetzle and gravy and a side of sauerkraut. The lady will have a schnitzel with a side of potato salad."

The man thanked us, took our menus, and walked away.

"I hope that's okay."

I was annoyed, but I reminded myself that he was probably trying to be helpful since I was new to German food. This afternoon, while I walked the streets of Austin, I thought about my situation. Although I saw a completely different side to him, and I doubted I'd ever be able to trust him, I wanted to make it work. I told myself to be patient and give him a chance. I wanted and needed answers and was determined to be more understanding.

"It's fine," I told him.

We looked at each other, and I knew the time had come.

"I've been thinking about what you said this morning."

"What part?"

"About your name."

"Yes?"

"I'm still not sure I understand."

He nodded and rolled his sleeves to the elbow, leaned back in his chair, and crossed his arms.

"What name did you register under in the hotel?" he asked.

"What?"

"In the Driskill. What name did you register with? I know it wasn't Louise Clifford. I asked for Louise Clifford's room, and they had nobody under that name."

I looked at him with my mouth open.

"You see? You've done the same thing, just perhaps on a smaller scale."

I hadn't thought of it that way, but as I considered it, relief washed over me.

"Why were you so angry when I approached you in the capitol? You hurt my wrist."

He extended his hand across the table, reaching for mine. I hesitated, but relented and gave it to him. He took it, turned it over, and kissed the inside of my wrist, brushing his lips against my skin. The movement sent electric jolts up my arm.

"I'm sorry," he said, his breath tickling my skin. He leaned back and placed my hand on the table. "I didn't mean to hurt you. But you yelled at me in front of many important business associates and called me a liar. Did you forget?"

I felt myself blush. "I did, didn't I?"

He winked at me. "You did."

Our host returned with two huge mugs of beer. The foam on the top must have been three or four inches. He placed them down in front of us. "I be back with food."

Charles laughed at my expression. "Do you like beer?"

"I don't know."

"Try it."

I gripped it with two hands and strained to raise it to my lips. He watched as I took a sip. I grimaced, and he laughed. He picked his up by the handle and raised it to his mouth. I watched as his Adam's apple bobbed up and down as he swallowed. I couldn't help the attraction I felt for him.

He set down the mug with a thud and smiled, the foam on his upper lip. "Mmmm."

I giggled.

The man returned with two heaping plates of food. Mine was a large piece of breaded meat and a potato mixture. I looked across at Charles, and he had a sausage, noodles with brown gravy over the top, and what must have been the sauerkraut. He took my plate and dished a portion of the sauerkraut onto it and handed it back. "Try it."

I picked up my fork and tentatively speared a piece, then put it in my mouth. I started chewing and regretted it. The smell and taste were too much for my feeble stomach, and I knew I was going to throw up. I leaped from the table and put my hand over my mouth. I ran toward a sign that said, "Ladies."

I threw open the door and ran to the toilet. I leaned over it and let loose, depositing everything I had inside me, along with the sauerkraut.

After several minutes, I trusted myself enough to stand and clean myself up. I was so embarrassed I considered sneaking out of the restaurant and walking back to the hotel, but knew I couldn't. When I returned to the table, I avoided looking at him. I could feel his eyes on me.

"Are you okay?" he asked.

"I'm sorry," I said as I sat down. "My condition makes me sensitive to tastes and smells."

I looked at him, and his eyes were so kind, so understanding. I saw no judgment.

"I'm sorry. I shouldn't have forced you."

I reached across the table, taking his hand. "It's okay. Really. I'm fine."

He continued to look at me, but I motioned with my hand, and he picked up his fork. He ate while I watched him.

"So, what should I call you?"

"What do you mean?"

"Do I call you Charles? Or Richard?"

He paused; his fork suspended over his plate. "Oh, well...in public, Richard. But if it's just us, whatever you like."

He winked, and I blushed. He continued to eat, then looked over at me. "Not hungry?"

I held my stomach. "I'm sorry."

He picked up his napkin from his lap and wiped at his mouth. "No, I understand."

He went on eating, devouring everything on his plate, then looked at mine. I shrugged, and he pulled the plate across the table. He ate it all, even finishing both beers. I watched him in amazement. *Where does he put it all?* He had a lean, muscular build. I'd seen him naked, and it was almost as if he didn't have an ounce of fat on him.

After he finished, he paid the bill, and we left. We walked out onto the quiet street, hand in hand. The streetlights were on, but otherwise, it was dark. I'd assumed, rather hoped, that would bring cooler temperatures, but the oven they called South Texas kept raging. It felt every bit as hot as midday. There just wasn't a sun.

"Is it always this hot?" I asked, squeezing his hand as we walked.

"It cools down for a few months in the wintertime. Between November and March. Most days are in the sixties."

"It never snows?"

"Rarely. I've never seen it."

I couldn't imagine a winter like that. It sounded glorious. I guess it was the trade-off for these stifling summers. The winters in Chicago brought feet of snow, and the wind blowing off Lake Michigan could kill a person if they stayed out in it long enough.

"Did you grow up here?"

His eyes were straight ahead as we walked, but now he looked at me. He shook his head. I didn't think so. I didn't hear the accent in his speech like I'd heard from others.

"Where then?"

"Colorado." That surprised me. "A little town called Colorado Springs."

"Hmm. What brought you here?"

He looked into my eyes. "What brought *you*?"

"I was looking for you."

He shrugged and looked away. "Okay, yes, but why did you leave Chicago?"

"I'm pregnant, remember?"

He shook his head. "You know as well as I do, you wanted to get away from your family. I was the same."

We'd reached my hotel now, and he escorted me inside. He angled toward the stairs, but I pulled him to the elevator. When we reached my floor and the operator wished us a good night, I handed him my key. He took it and unlocked the door. He stood at the threshold, looking into my eyes, the blue bright as the sky at midday. I walked through the door and turned back to look at him. He stared into my eyes, stepped inside, and shut the door behind him.

Chapter 22

Michael

At five-thirty, Michael goes downstairs and sits in a lobby chair across from the registration desk. The clerk he spoke with earlier notices him and, after registering a couple from St. Louis, calls him over. Michael stands and approaches the desk. The clerk leans forward.

"Are you waiting for Mr. Fredricks?"

"Yes."

"You know, one problem with being a hotel clerk, beyond smiling all day, is that the pay is less than desirable. Sometimes I accept opportunities to make a little extra when the amount is right."

Michael eyes him. "What do you have in mind?"

"Me? Nothing. I only accept or decline invitations."

Michael nods. "I have an extra dime in my pocket."

"Oh, for something that small, the request would have to be minimal."

"How about when Mr. Fredricks comes in, you point him out to me?" Michael assumes Fredricks won't be hard to identify, but for a dime, it wouldn't hurt to keep the clerk happy and on his side.

"Make it a quarter and you've got a deal."

Michael smiles and shakes his head, sliding the dime across the desk. The man watches him, then takes it, and waves Michael back to his chair.

Twenty minutes pass, and a man in a substantial cowboy hat walks through the door. Michael's attention is drawn to him, not because of the hat, but the entire outfit. Everything is white, even the cowboy boots. Only his belt buckle and bolo tie aren't. Both are black. The man notices Michael watching him and tips his hat, then crosses the lobby to the clerk.

"Nice to see you today, Mr. Fredricks."

"Howdy, Roy. How's the day been?"

"Not bad. Only one empty room tonight."

"Excellent."

The two exit the lobby, ducking inside an office behind the desk. After a couple of minutes, Fredricks exits with Roy behind him. Roy looks at Michael and indicates with his head, as if Michael didn't already know the man was Fredricks.

"Well, goodnight. See you tomorrow," he says to Roy without turning around. He walks toward the exit, tips his hat again to Michael, and exits. Michael stands and follows him out.

For an older man, Fredricks moves quickly. He's half a block down the road when Michael exits, and he has to hurry to catch up. As he approaches, Fredricks whirls around and aims a pistol in Michael's face. Michael steps back, raising his hands.

"Whoa."

"You picked the wrong man to rob, partner."

Michael shakes his head and takes another step back. "Listen, I don't want to rob you. I just want to ask you a few questions about Richard Amhurst."

Fredricks lowers his weapon from Michael's head to his chest.

"Amhurst? What about him?"

"I understand you found him in Kansas City. I've been looking for him as well. Mayor Brown said I should talk to you."

Fredricks holsters his gun and eyes Michael.

"Buy me a drink, and you can ask anything you like."

Five minutes later, they sit at the bar in The Lonestar Saloon. Fredricks orders a whiskey and Michael a beer. After the bartender serves them, Fredricks takes a sip and looks at Michael.

"What do you want to know?"

"Everything you can tell me about Amhurst."

Fredricks holds the glass in his hand, moving it from side to side, the whiskey jostling with each movement.

"Why? What's in it for you? Does he owe you money, too?"

"I'm a detective from Denver. He matches the description of someone I'm looking for."

"Who?"

"A man named Thomas Slater."

"What makes you think it's him?"

"Mostly his physical description. Slater was tall, lean, late twenties, with dark hair, and piercing blue eyes. It's the eyes that stand out. Slater was last seen headed east. Kansas City is east of Denver."

Fredricks takes another drink of his whiskey. "What'd he do? Why you after him?"

"Murdered his wife."

Fredricks chews on his cheek, then takes a drink and slams down the glass.

"Charlie? Another one."

The bartender comes over and refills his cup.

"I first met Richard Amhurst two years ago. Claimed he was from some town Indiana way. I could tell he wasn't a Texan. He talked like a northerner. Indiana made as much sense as anywhere." Fredricks raises a hand and flips it. "A friend of mine introduced him to me. Said he was looking for an investor in a hotel. Promised great returns. I'd just sold me a piece of land and had some money in my pocket. Seemed like a perfect fit. I liked him. He was a gentleman and had a good head on his shoulders. Smart."

Fredricks takes a drink.

"He was fixin' to build a hotel and needed a partner. He was gonna run everything, and all I had to do was give him fifteen thousand bucks. He knew someone who drew up the contract, and I signed and handed him the cash. I didn't look at the contract closely, not sure I could understand it if I did. Well, it turns out I was never partners with Richard Amhurst, but a man by the name of Charles Watson."

Fredricks turns and points at Michael. His eyes have a shiny aspect to them now.

"But there was more to it. Amhurst got another loan from some big-shot fellers back in New York City. Thirty thousand. They didn't know about me. And I didn't know about them. But they weren't partners with Watson, they were partners with Amhurst. We was both partners in the same hotel with a different person."

"So, what happened? How'd you find out?"

"Amhurst split. Took the money and ran. He didn't pay any of the contractors that done built the hotel. Just kept putting them off, complaining about this or that. Promising to pay when things were fixed. But they never were, and he was never fixin' to pay them in the first place."

"And he just left town?"

Fredricks nods.

"Hmm, so it was the money that made him leave?"

"That's how it looked. But I think there was even more to it."

"Oh?"

Fredricks nods. "I think it had something to do with his wife. Married a young thing from Chicago, maybe? Claimed he knew her from back home. She got knocked up, and then nobody done seen her again. Folks think she split town, and he went chasing after her."

"But you don't?"

Fredricks shakes his head. "No...I think he left before he was ready. Something happened."

"Like what?"

"You said you been looking for Amhurst because he killed his wife?"

Michael nods.

"I think he did it again."

"He killed her?"

Fredricks takes a drink of his whiskey and shrugs.

"What makes you think that?"

"Amhurst had a business meetin' set up with another investor. That fellar was fixin' to pay him double what I paid. Knowin' him, no way he'd scoot away from that unless he was forced. She did somethin', and he killed her for it, then had to run."

Michael nods and takes a drink of his beer. "So, what happened after he left?"

Fredricks shakes his head. "After he disappeared, they come after me, the contractors. The only way I could hold them off was promisin' to run the hotel and pay them from the profits. Not long after I started runnin' it, a man from back east way visited me. That's when I learnt about the other investors."

Michael sits back on his barstool and takes a chug from his beer. "Amhurst is in jail now. Where's the money?"

Fredricks throws up his hands. "I don't know. He wouldn't talk in that jail. He hid it someplace. Not sure where. You said you saw him in Kansas City?"

"Yes."

"Clam up? Still won't say a thing?"

Michael nods.

"It's someplace. Boy, I wish I could find it. It'd solve all my problems."

Chapter 23

Louise

"How are you feeling, Louise?"

I swung my legs down and sat on the bed I shared with my husband, pulling my dress back down. The doctor stepped away, having just conducted his weekly examination.

It was two months since Richard and I had been married, and my pregnancy was no longer a secret. Every day, I looked down and thought someone was pushing air into my stomach. It just kept expanding. Richard didn't trust hospitals and paid extra money for the doctor to make house calls. It was nice seeing how much Richard cared for me and the baby. He was wonderful. Whenever he was around, he was such a doting husband. He just wasn't around much.

"I'm okay."

I squirmed under the doctor's watchful glance.

"How have you been eating?"

"Fine."

"Are you still struggling to keep your food down?"

"No, not as much."

He made a note in his notepad and sat in the chair near the window, crossing his legs.

"Tell me what you've been eating."

"Fruits, vegetables, everything you tell me."

His eyes narrowed, and I wondered if he could tell I was lying.

"You need meat. Protein is very important for a pregnant woman. What about dairy? Milk? Cheese?"

I nodded.

"This week I want you to keep a journal. I want to know everything you've eaten and when. Do you have a notebook?"

"Yes." I pointed to one on the side of our bed on the nightstand.

"Good." He uncrossed his legs and prepared to stand, but stopped. "What about emotionally? How has that been going?"

"Fine."

He peered at me more closely, and I squirmed.

"Have you been walking?"

I started to answer, but stopped myself. I might be able to lie to him once and get away with it, but twice was pushing it. It's not like I had a beautiful tan. My skin was white as chalk. I realized he was asking a question to which he already knew the answer. It was a test. It didn't take Sherlock Holmes to see the pallor of my skin and the pile of books next to the bed and in our front room to see I'd rather read than get exercise. I shook my head.

He frowned, disappointment written all over his face. "Louise, it's very important that you walk each day. Two miles, that's all I ask. Will you promise me?"

I sighed. "But it's so hot out there. I get out in that sun, and I just want to melt."

"Go early in the morning or later in the evening. Sometime when it's cooler. You need some sun, but the walk is most important."

I suppressed a laugh at, "sometime when it's cooler." Summer in South Texas, there wasn't a cooler. I coughed, then nodded, and he stood. I walked him to the front door and saw him out. I watched as he walked down the stairs and out onto the street. He climbed into his automobile and drove away. I looked up at the sky, through the window, and told myself to go on a walk. I tried telling myself to open the door and follow his path away from the house. But I didn't. Instead, I picked up my current book, *The Count of Monte Cristo,* and plopped down on the couch.

After reading for a couple of hours, I put the book down and rummaged around in the kitchen for something to eat. I looked at the vegetables Richard had brought home yesterday but couldn't bring myself to include them. Instead, I picked up a pastry.

Five minutes later, a feeling of guilt took hold, and I resolved to follow one of the doctor's commands. I changed my shoes, placed a hat on my head, and walked out the door. I strolled along the street, occasionally nodding and smiling at people I passed. One woman I'd seen before, but the rest were strangers. I'd been in Austin for two months and knew only three people. Richard, the doctor, and Carol, the old woman next door. Although people were friendly, I found it difficult to make conversation. I would have rather read a conversation than take part in one. I was always that way, but I thought I was getting worse.

I had gone several blocks, and the heat of the sun was baking me. I felt perspiration under my arms, and a bead of sweat rolled down my back. I noticed a park across the street with large trees and several benches. The allure of the shade pulled me, and I headed toward one of them. I sat and looked around. I wished I had brought my book. The park was relatively quiet, other than an occasional carriage or automobile passing on the street.

After several minutes, I returned home. The park was only less than a mile from home, but at least I had gotten outside. A woman, maybe a couple of years older than me, entered the park and walked along the stone path. She was coming toward me but had yet to notice. She was tall and lean, with light-colored hair pulled back in a braid. When she was less than ten feet from me, she finally looked up and saw me. I smiled, and she smiled back.

"Hello," she said.

"Hello."

I expected her to continue along her path, but she didn't. Instead, she sat down on the park bench next to me.

"I'm Mary Tuberville."

She wasn't looking at me. Instead, her eyes were focused on the park. She raised an elbow and placed it on the bench behind us. She was wearing a light pastel summer dress. There was something familiar about her, but I couldn't place it.

"I'm Barbara." I started to say the last name I had used in the hotel, Johansson, but caught myself and said, Amhurst.

"Amhurst," she said. "Richard Amhurst?"

I nodded. "Yes, he's my husband."

She chuckled. "So, you're the famous Mrs. Amhurst?"

I looked at her, confused.

She reached over and patted my shoulder. "I just say that because ever since your husband came to town, he's been the object of attention for many women. The new eligible bachelor and all that. Nobody thought he'd settle down until you came along."

"Sorry to disappoint you."

"Oh, I wasn't one of them. I mean, my father likes Richard, and hinted that we should see each other, but I've never been good at doing what he tells me."

I could relate to that.

We sat on the bench, neither of us looking at the other, when she asked, "So, where's home for you?"

"Chicago."

"Illinois?"

"Yes, unless there's another one I'm unaware of."

She laughed, and I smiled.

"I've never been. Never even been outside of Texas."

"It feels like another planet from here."

"How so?"

I cocked my head to the side, wondering how I might explain it to her. "Let's just say there are thousands more people and it's not as hot."

She held a fan and waved it back and forth in front of her face. "That sounds nice about now. Did you meet Richard there?"

"Yes."

"And he brought you to Texas?"

"In a manner of speaking."

"What did your family think of that?"

I looked away.

"What? They don't know?"

I shook my head.

"But why?"

I took a deep breath and looked out over the park. "Richard was supposed to marry my sister." I shrugged. "He liked me better."

"And you ran away with him..."

I nodded.

She smiled. "I knew I liked you."

I laughed and stretched out on the bench.

"And you haven't tried to contact them? Tell them where you are?"

I shook my head. "I can't. It's hard to explain."

She looked at me and I saw her eyes lower.

"When's that baby due?"

"Seven months."

It was actually five, but I was sure she could do basic math.

"That's going to be a big baby."

"That's what I'm told."

"Maybe twins."

A lurch of fear gripped me, but then I remembered I wasn't really as big as I seemed. I held my hands under the bump in my stomach. It was a position I found myself holding more and more often. Although I liked her and didn't want to leave, I also didn't want to answer more questions about myself and Richard. I tried to turn the conversation to her.

"So, you're born and raised here?"

She nodded.

"How long have you known Richard?"

"About two years. My father introduced us not long after he arrived."

"Who's your father?"

"John Tuberville. He serves on the city council. He's a lawyer."

I looked at her, and remembrance came into my mind. I knew where I'd seen her before. She was in the capitol the night I had called Richard a liar. I felt myself blush and looked away.

"What is it?" she asked.

"You were there."

A mischievous smile appeared on her face. "Where?"

"The capitol."

She chuckled. "I was."

I put a hand to my cheek, sweating profusely.

"Don't be like that. I wish I had that kind of courage. Plus, you provided some excellent entertainment and gossip. And it worked to get Claire Leishman's claws out of him. I wondered if that's why you did it."

Hearing that my behavior that night was a topic of gossip in town embarrassed me further. I only knew three people, but everyone knew me. That explained some looks I got when I ventured out, the knowing smiles.

"Who's Claire Leishman?"

"The woman Richard was with that night. He had his arm around her when you started screaming. Wasn't it about her?"

"I was just surprised."

"Judging by the look on her face, so was she. After Richard came back, they left soon after. But you're the girl who won, right?"

"Won? What do you mean?"

"Richard. You're the one who ended up with him. He picked you. She's gone now, anyway. It all worked out."

We talked for a few more minutes, then Mary said she had to go, and we planned to meet again in a few days. I walked home, plopped down on the couch, and picked up my book. But I couldn't focus on the words. From the time Richard had come to the hotel the day after the capitol, he had been the Charles I knew in Chicago. My jealousy toward the other woman he had held that night diminished to the point I stopped thinking about her. But hearing Mary talk about her stoked the fire again. I wanted to know what had been going on between them and what had happened to her.

Chapter 24

Louise

Richard got home late that night. Before marrying him, I had cooked nothing. I grew up with a housekeeper and a cook. My mother always said that if she raised us right, we'd never have to cook. She knew how, but she never taught us. I think she thought it was beneath us.

After marrying Richard, I found myself severely lacking in the domesticated wife role. Especially when it came to dinner. Clueless about where and how to start, I bought a cookbook and spent the first day practicing before he came home. When he arrived, I had the table set and served him. I watched him take the first bite and smile. I thought he truly enjoyed it. While he took another bite, I served myself and sampled it. It was awful. It was everything I could do not to spit it back out. I looked over at him, knowing there was no way he could like it. Even then, he didn't admit that he hated it. I had to pry it out of him, eventually taking the plate away. He was so skillful in his deception that I believed him.

Knowing he was a good liar was nothing new. I had watched him with my family in Chicago. He had told them things I knew to be false, and he did it so naturally. Eventually, we ate sandwiches and laughed about my first attempt. That night, holding each other in bed, I made him promise not to lie about the food again. I gave him my word I'd practice, and I'd never serve him anything I hadn't tasted first. He agreed. Afterward, I told him that no lying extended to everything, not just cooking. We could get through anything if we were honest and open with each other.

Since then, I hadn't a reason to believe he'd lied to me. Tonight, I would test him.

"Richard," I said, looking at him across the table, "what's your real name?"

He looked at me, his fork full of chicken. "What?"

"Your name. Everyone here calls you Richard. In Chicago, you were Charles. I know why you did it and why you want me to call you Richard now. But I'm your wife. We promised to keep no secrets between us. I want to know your real name."

He set down his fork and rubbed his chin. This morning, he woke late and left the house before shaving. By now, it probably felt like sandpaper. Two days of growth would certainly make him scratchy.

"Why does it matter?"

I eyed him. He was stalling. "I want to be close to you."

He frowned. "We are close."

"I know. But I want nothing between us."

He hesitated, and I lost patience. I stood from the table and scraped the food into the garbage. I dropped my plate into the sink, but before I could exit the kitchen, he walked to me. He wrapped me in his arms and held me. At first, I struggled against him, but I eventually gave in. After a moment, he tipped my head up to look at him.

"Samuel."

I smiled. "See? Was that so hard? Samuel what?"

"Bruner."

I went up on tiptoes and kissed him, then pulled him down the hall to our bedroom.

Thirty minutes later, I lie in bed looking up at the ceiling while his breathing grew slow and deep. Before long, he was softly snoring beside me. I turned and looked at him in the dark. He lay on his side, facing me. After coming home from the park, I couldn't stop thinking about my conversation with Mary. She had told me that the woman he was dating before I had arrived left town. But why? She was born and raised here. Why would she leave?

Was it because she was embarrassed that he chose me over her? I doubted it. Something didn't seem right about the story. I couldn't let it rest. I had to learn more. I went to the cellar, searching for something, anything, to help me learn more about my husband. I found a box, and inside was a photograph. It was a picture from many years ago of a man and a little boy. He couldn't have been over twelve years old, but I recognized him immediately. The man looked eerily similar to Richard now. It had to be his father. I stared at it, not thinking much of it until I turned it over. On the back, there was a handwritten inscription. *Phil and Thomas Colorado Springs, Colorado.*

Richard had failed my test, and I couldn't help but wonder what else that might mean.

Chapter 25

Michael

Michael enters the courthouse at the corner of Eleventh Street and Congress Avenue. It's a yellow brick building constructed just a few years before. It serves as both the courthouse and the jail. After introducing himself and asking for directions, he's pointed down the hall to the marshal's office. Years ago, the City of Austin had created its own police force and taken the city's jurisdiction from the county sheriff.

When he reaches the office door, Michael knocks without a reply. He looks down the hall and sees two more offices. He approaches each, reading the names on the doors. Both belong to judges. He considers knocking and asking about the marshal, but decides against it. When he turns back, Michael sees a man coming down the hall toward him. He's young, late twenties, with an average height and build. He wears a police uniform and is holding a cup of coffee. He notices Michael watching him and slows his pace.

"Can I help you?"

"Marshal Tilghman. Do you know him?"

"I've heard the name and seen the face a time or two."

"Are you him?"

"How'd you guess?"

They stand in the narrow hallway, barely wide enough for two grown men.

"My name is Michael Delaney. I'm a detective from Denver. I've come investigating a man who called himself Richard Amhurst."

The marshal's eyebrows raise, and his upper lip curls.

"Is that a fact?"

He motions with his head for Michael to follow and opens his office door with his free hand. Michael enters behind him.

"Coffee?" the marshal asks.

Typically, he wouldn't bother, but Michael feels himself dragging. "Yes, thank you."

"Be right back. Have a seat."

He motions to the only chair in the office not directly behind the desk and walks out. Michael surveys the room. One wall is adorned with the head of a four-point deer. The opposite wall features a painting of a magnificent nature scene—a chiseled mountain peak with a lake and elk in the foreground. Missing home, Michael steps closer to examine it. In the bottom-left corner, he finds a signature highlighting its creator: *H. Burns '98.*

The door opens, and the marshal walks in, a coffee cup in each hand. He extends one to Michael, and he takes it, thanking him.

"My wife's father painted that." He points with the hand still gripping his cup.

"Beautiful. Where is it?"

"Your neck of the woods. Somewhere in Colorado."

"Hmm. It looks familiar."

"Might be Denver."

He circles the desk and sits in the seat behind it. Michael rests his cup on the polished surface and pulls the other chair away from the wall. He sits across the desk from the marshal and picks up his cup.

"So, Amhurst?"

Michael nods.

"What about him? Did he show up in Colorado?"

"No, Kansas City."

The marshal raises an eyebrow.

Michael tells him about the prisoner in the Kansas City jail. About talking with the sheriff and the mayor and about the information they got from Mr. Fredricks.

"It's the mayor who told me to come to Austin. He thought I might learn more from Fredricks. I found Fredricks, and he told me several new things. That's why I've come to you."

"What did he tell you?"

"That Amhurst was married here in Austin. He thinks he killed his wife."

The marshal leans back, nodding and pulling at his lip. "Did he tell you why he thinks that?"

"He said he doesn't know. Says that she disappeared, and nobody heard from her again. He thinks Amhurst killed her."

"I think he's right. But it's hard to prove. Amhurst is a slick devil. If he did, he did a masterful job covering it up. We couldn't find any evidence of it. But I'm curious. Why do you care?"

"Because he did the same thing in Denver."

"Really?"

"He was going by a different name, but he matches the physical description of a dead woman's husband."

"So, you found the body?"

Michael takes a sip of his coffee and leans forward.

"He buried her in a farmer's field. It was luck that she was found. It could have been years, decades before anyone came across it. A man bought a new plot of land and found some disturbed dirt on his lot. He dug it up and found the body."

"Hmm. We haven't been so fortunate." The marshal leans forward over his desk. "Fredricks is right. He was married. But that's not all. His wife had a baby."

"Yeah, I heard that."

The marshal nods. "Had a baby and then disappeared. She hasn't been seen since."

"What about the baby?"

He shakes his head. "Mother and child vanished. She was from someplace in Chicago. Unfortunately, we couldn't track her down. No woman matching her description was reported missing in Chicago. We don't even know her name. The name on the marriage license doesn't match any birth records in the Chicago area. We tried to find her and Amhurst, but hit dead ends everywhere we looked."

Michael leans back and sighs.

"What was the name on the marriage license?"

"For her?"

"Yes."

"Barbara Johansson. The only Barbara Johansson we could find in Chicago that was even close is still there, married, with three kids. That was it, no other leads."

Michael stands, having finished his coffee. "I appreciate your time, Marshal."

The marshal stands and walks him out. Michael opens the door and turns back around to shake his hand, but the marshal has one last thing to say.

"Detective?"

"Yes?"

"I think he killed two other women while he was here. There's no proof, and the bodies have never been found, but he did it. If there's anything I can do to help you nail him, don't hesitate."

Chapter 26

Louise

I sat on the bench, scanning the park, when I saw with delight my new friend Mary Tuberville walking toward me. It had been a week since we had met, and I'd been here every day since, hoping I'd run into her. Each day I'd left disappointed, but it certainly helped convince the doctor I was doing all he told me.

When she reached me, she slumped down on the bench like someone had taken out her knees. Within seconds, she took off her shoes and leaned back, resting both arms on the back of the bench.

"I've got a bone to pick with you, you know?"

A nervous flutter rippled through me, and I wondered what she knew. Her eyes remained shut as her head rested on the bench, her face aimed at the sky. She opened an eye, checking to see if I was listening.

"You haven't screamed at anyone since you first got here. You've been boring, and I don't like it."

I chuckled, and she opened her eyes and looked at me.

"I'm serious. I'm so bored. Life's more exciting when you yell at someone. I'm not asking you to physically fight. Maybe just a shouting match or two. Preferably in a public forum."

Suddenly, my feet felt claustrophobic in my shoes as I watched her toes run along the grass. I joined her, removing my sandals and letting my soles brush the cool grass. She opened her eyes wide and sat up, pulling her legs under herself.

"I think you've grown since the last time I saw you. What are you feeding that child?"

I know she didn't mean it as an insult, but that morning, as I looked at myself in the mirror, I cried. Weight had always been an issue for me, as my mother had constantly reminded me. But looking in the mirror and seeing the roundness of my belly, the widening of my hips, it was hard, and now having a virtual stranger point it out...

"Nice to see you, too," I said sarcastically. Doing my best to fight back.

She curled a smile. "Thank you."

She pushed my arm, the behavior reminding me of my sister. Tears came to my eyes. She saw it and frowned.

"Hey...I didn't mean it. I was just having some fun."

I turned away, unable to stop the tears. She put a hand on my back.

"Hey, what's wrong? What is it?"

I remained turned away from her, tears streaming down my face, her hand resting on my back. After a minute, I pulled myself together and wiped the tears from my eyes. I took a few big breaths, then turned back to look at her.

"I'm sorry. I'm not even sure why I'm crying. My emotions are all over the place."

She looked at me with concern but said nothing, patting my shoulder. I forced a smile, and she didn't return it but removed her hand. She went back to resting her arms on the top of the bench while I sat with my hands in my lap, looking at the dirt path in front of us.

"I did mean it," I said, trying to smooth the awkwardness that had arisen. "It is good to see you."

"You too. Sorry, I was just playing. I mean, you are as big as a house, but I shouldn't have said it."

I laughed. "Oh, I know. But listen, I'm glad you're here. There was something I wanted to ask you."

Her eyes were closed again, her head resting back against the bench. "Shoot."

"Last time we talked, you said that the woman Richard was with, what was her name?"

"Claire Leishman."

"Yes, Claire. You said it doesn't matter now because she's gone, anyway. What did you mean by that?"

"Oh, nothing. Claire left. Moved away."

"Why?"

She shrugged. "I guess she was so ashamed by Richard choosing you, she couldn't handle it. She was gone, and her parents started looking for her, then a telegram came in from Dallas. Claire said she was so ashamed that she couldn't stay anymore. She left town, deciding to start a new life."

The news brought relief, but strangely, it brought disappointment as well. Of course, I wanted nothing to happen to the girl. But if something had, it would have brought validation to my concerns. As if I was justified in thinking the thoughts I had about Richard.

Mary opened her eyes and sat forward. "I couldn't believe it when I heard it. I mean, I've known Claire since we were kids. She was incredibly proud, always had to have the prettiest dress, and always had to be the envy of the other kids. That part I believe. I'm sure she was ashamed and devastated by Richard choosing you. But moving away on her own? No way. I just can't believe she did that. Something isn't right."

"What do you mean?"

"Look at you, for instance. You grew up in Chicago and came here with nobody but Richard. That takes a tremendous amount of courage. Claire would never do that. She's the type of girl who couldn't do anything on her own. She never left the house without someone else. Now you're telling me she moved across the state on her own? I don't buy it."

I felt a strange mixture of excitement and terror.

"Well then, what happened to her?"

She threw up her hands. "I don't know. Maybe someone helped her. I just know she didn't do it on her own."

We talked for several more minutes before Mary stood abruptly. "I forgot. I'm late for something." Without waiting for me to reply, she turned and strode away, but stopped. "You know you're really not, right?"

"What?"

"Big as a house."

"What?"

"I was just teasing you. You're still beautiful, even with a few extra pounds."

Later that night, when Richard came home, I had dinner prepared for him. The table was set, just like he liked it, and I greeted him with a kiss and showed him to his seat. I poured him a beer and told him dinner would be ready shortly.

On our first night together in Austin, he had taken me to a German restaurant. I figured that type of food must have been his favorite, although he hadn't told me so. My cookbook had a recipe for sauerbraten, and I worked all afternoon and evening to get it right.

I picked sauerbraten because, although similar in name to sauerkraut, it didn't have any in it. Even the memory of that night made my stomach roll. When I started cooking, I worried that the smell of German food might send my stomach back into convulsions but, thankfully, it didn't. My nausea had lessened recently. I imagined it was one of the few advantages of having a larger stomach.

After serving Richard, I served myself a small amount and sat across the table from him.

"How was your day?" I asked, keeping the conversation light. I needed time to warm to the chief topic.

"Fine," he said, looking at the meal on his plate. "German food?"

"Is that okay? I thought maybe you liked it since you took me to a German place on my first night here."

"I do." He eyed the food with skepticism.

"What?"

He looked up and smiled. "Nothing, it's just that...have you ever made anything like this before?"

"What? Do you think I'd ruin it? Too difficult to make?"

"No, it's just...it doesn't seem easy."

"Try it. If you don't like it, you don't have to eat it."

He picked up his fork and speared the beef, cautiously putting it in his mouth. I watched as he chewed thoughtfully. A genuine smile broke out across his face.

"Wow!" He chuckled and speared more meat.

I couldn't help the giggle that erupted from me. "You like it?"

"Yeah," he said and laughed.

He devoured everything on his plate and asked for more. I served him all I had, and he ate it in no time. When he finished, he leaned back, holding his beer with a contented look.

"Richard?"

"Hmm?"

"I have something I want to ask you."

"Yes?"

"Would it be okay if I went to visit my family in Chicago?"

His beer was held to his lips, his Adam's apple bouncing up and down as he swallowed. He froze. His eyes were on me.

"I just think it's important I go now. I left so suddenly, without saying goodbye. They don't even know where I am. If I don't go now, with the baby coming, I don't know when I'd be able to."

He put his beer on the table and sat up. "Louise, I can't go now. The hotel just opened. I need to be here for a while."

"Oh, I know. I wasn't thinking you would go. I think it would be better for me to go and explain to them why I left and where I am now. I'm sure they're worried. My conscience hasn't been able to rest since I came here."

He shook his head. "Louise, I don't think that's a good idea. I'm not sending my pregnant wife across the country on her own."

"I came here on my own," I said with a hint of anger in my voice. "Remember?"

"You weren't as pregnant then."

"My health was worse. I couldn't keep anything down. How often have you seen me throw up now?"

He leaned forward, his elbows on the table. "Where is this coming from? I thought you hated your mother. I thought you wanted to be as far away from them as possible."

I sighed. "I did. But...I don't know. I guess these last few months have changed my mind. Maybe it's because I'm becoming a mother myself. But I know it's something I have to do."

He rubbed the top of his head, twisting his wavy, dark hair. He hadn't said it, but I sensed a change.

"I won't be gone longer than two weeks. I'll be back in plenty of time before the baby comes, and Dr. Frieberg told me he thinks it will be fine."

"Dr. Frieberg said that?"

I nodded, and he scrutinized my face for a long time before finally saying, "Okay."

Chapter 27

Louise

My seat vibrated, and I looked out the window. After boarding, the rhythmic slide of the train scurrying down the track put me to sleep. I leaned against the window and conked out.

I woke with my face plastered to the glass, a small amount of spittle running from my mouth. I didn't know how long I was out or what time it was. Two days before leaving Austin, I had broken my watch, and the repairman said it would be at least a week before he could fix it.

As I stared out the window, I panicked, worrying I had missed my stop. The weather in Austin was bright and sunny, but here, wherever that was, it was dark and gloomy, with rain falling in buckets. The landscape was no longer zooming past, and we were slowing down. I'd never been on a train when it was raining and it made me wonder. *Is a downpour like this bad for a train? Do they lose traction and slide off the tracks if there's too much water? Maybe that's why we're stopping.*

People around me rose from their seats and loaded their bags, preparing to disembark. I looked back out the window and pressed my face to the glass, searching for any sign that might tell me where I was. It wasn't long before I saw a large, white sign with black block letters showing *Kansas City*. I could hardly believe my eyes. A few months ago, when I did this trip in reverse, it felt like we'd never reach Taylor Station from here. Now, I fell asleep, and the next thing I knew, I was there.

I sat and waited patiently, eager to disembark but unwilling to fight the jostling bodies and protruding elbows. When most of the car cleared, I stood, retrieved my bag, and walked to the exit. A train attendant saw me and stepped forward.

"Can I take that for you, ma'am?"

He extended his arm, reached for the bag, and I gave it to him. Then I followed him off the train. When he handed it back to me, I thanked him. As I walked away, I wondered about his choice of words. It was the first time anyone had ever called me "ma'am." Up to then, I was always "miss." Was it the ring on my left hand? Or maybe my protruding belly? I was younger than he was. Something about it unsettled me. It made me wonder about the change of just three months. When I had left Chicago in search of Charles, I didn't know where I was going or if I'd find him. I was uncertain and scared about my future. Now, I was every bit as unsettled, but for a different reason.

I reached the line at the ticket counter and looked up on the departures board. I saw cities like Cleveland, Detroit, Memphis, St. Louis, Chicago, Denver, and Santa Fe. One particular city caught my eye. Something bumped my shoulder, pulling me from my trance. I turned around to see an older gentleman with a mustache that went around his mouth, looking down at me. He made a motion with his hand, and I turned back to see the ticket agent waiting for me.

"Next in line," she said, scowling at me.

I stepped up to the counter.

"Um...," I said and stepped back to look up at the board again.

"Ma'am, where do you want to go?"

There it was again. I looked back at her, debating, then decided.

"One ticket to Colorado Springs, please?"

Chapter 28

Michael

Michael Delaney enters the Cook County courthouse in Chicago, Illinois, and looks around. This is the furthest north and east he's ever been, and the size of the city overwhelms him. Like everything in Chicago, the lobby of the courthouse is busy with people scurrying around. Unlike the smaller towns of Austin and Kansas City, this courthouse includes a sign showing where each office is located. After consulting the sign, he walks up the stairs two levels and enters a room with *County Clerk* etched on the glass.

"Can I help you?" a lovely, young woman with curly, blond hair and bright-blue eyes asks from behind a desk in the front of the large room full of cabinets.

"Yes, hello. My name is Detective Delaney from Denver, Colorado. I'm conducting a criminal investigation and need your help. What's your name?"

She smiles. "I'm Sandra."

"Hi, Sandra. Has anyone ever told you that you have the most beautiful eyes?"

"Thank you," she says, blushing.

"Do you think you could help me?"

□"Well, that depends. But I'll sure try."

"Thank you. I need to examine the birth records for all babies born about twenty years ago with the name of Barbara. Would that be possible?"

Sandra stands from the desk and bobs her head enthusiastically. "Yes. It won't be easy, but I could do that. Do you have any other information about them? Address or part of the city? Parents' names? Anything at all?"

"No, sorry. That's all I have. I'm looking for a Barbara in her early twenties from Chicago. I wish I had more."

"Oh, okay, no problem. Well, make yourself comfortable. It's going to be a little while. If you want to have a seat in that chair, I'll be back as soon as I can."

She turns to walk away, and Michael moves to the chair, but she stops and spins around.

"Umm...I'm sorry, but I have to ask: what's this for?"

Michael smiles. "I'm a detective investigating a missing person's case."

Her eyes go wide. "Oh, okay." She turns to leave, but stops again. "I'm really very sorry. But do you have some form of identification? It's just that I could get in trouble."

Michael pulls his police badge from his pocket and flashes it at her.

"Great! Thank you so much. I'll be back as soon as I can."

"Take your time."

Michael sits in the chair near the door and waits.

After forty minutes, Sandra returns with a file full of papers.

"Here they are. You can't take them with you, but I can clear off this table, and you can look them over."

Michael sits in the chair, and Sandra places them on the table in front of him.

"If you can, please keep them in the same order. I'm going to have to put them all back, and it will be easier for me that way."

"Of course."

"I'll just be over here if you need me."

"Thank you."

Michael opens the file and starts examining each birth record. He's not sure what he's looking for, but assumes he'll know if he finds it. When he was in Austin, the marshal had said the wife of Richard was listed as Barbara Johansson on the marriage license. The marshal had said they looked for someone matching the name, but nobody in Chicago matched, other than one woman with three kids. Out of leads, the marshal had given up looking. Michael had to wonder, what if the names meant something? What if they weren't pulled from thin air?

He knows it's a long shot, and maybe the girl wasn't even from Chicago and he's barking up the wrong tree. But he needs to try.

After flipping through ten records, he stops. The date of birth matches, but it's the mother's maiden name that gets his blood pumping. He picks up the record and walks back to Sandra. "Excuse me, Sandra?"

"Yes."

"Could you tell me where this woman lives now?"

Sandra takes the record from him and examines it. "If there's a property under her name, I can. Would you like me to look?"

"Yes, please."

Sandra leaves again and comes back five minutes later, frowning.

"Sorry, no properties under her name. But I found one for her parents. They live in Oak Park. Close to here."

Chapter 29

Louise

The house looked like it could be on the front page of any magazine promoting small-town America. The buggy driver told me it would only take fifteen minutes from the hotel, and he was right. It was a beautiful, bright summer day. The air was clean and light. When I first arrived two days ago, I could feel the elevation. I was always short of breath. It was as if less oxygen was entering my lungs each time I inhaled. I thought maybe it was the baby growing larger and pressing against my lungs. But a woman in the hotel noticed me laboring to breathe after climbing the stairs and came over. She asked if I would be okay, and I told her I would and that it was just the pregnancy. She asked where I was from, and when I told her Austin, she laughed. She told me Colorado Springs was over six thousand feet above sea level and the oxygen level was far less than home. That knowledge relieved me. I was concerned that something was wrong. She told me not to worry, this being my first pregnancy. It was natural for me to overthink things.

"Would you like me to wait?"

The carriage driver looked down at me from his seat. I exited the buggy and stood on the dirt road in front of the farmhouse.

"If you don't mind. Just until I'm sure someone is home."

He nodded, and I turned back to the house and walked up the path leading to the front door. The house was a large two-story structure with a wraparound porch and a swing. Mountains rose from behind the house, and I could barely see the nearest neighbor. I walked up the steps leading to the front door and knocked.

After a few seconds, a grandmotherly woman in a blue housedress stared at me through the screen door.

"Mrs. Slater?"

"Yes?"

"My name is Barbara Johansson."

"Yes."

"I wondered if I might talk to you for a few minutes."

She opened the screen door and joined me on the porch. She looked at my driver, and he waved at her.

"What about?"

"I understand Thomas Slater is your nephew."

She looked away from my driver and back at me. Her eyes narrowed, and she wiped her hands on her apron. "You can come in." She opened the screen door and held it for me. "I'm baking some bread. We can talk in the kitchen."

I waved to the driver and entered the home. To my right was a small room with an upright piano, a couch, and two end tables with lamps. A fireplace was on the far wall. She paused in front of the room, then changed her mind and walked down the hallway past the staircase to the back of the house, and I followed. A large table with six chairs sat opposite the cooking area, and she pulled out one chair. "Have a seat. I need to check the oven."

I followed her command while she walked to the oven, opened the door, and looked inside. The smell of fresh bread permeated the space, and I felt a rumble in my stomach. Recently, I had felt the baby move, and sometimes it was hard to tell if it was the baby or hunger making the rumble. She closed the door and returned to the table, sitting down in the chair opposite me. She was a large woman with gigantic hands covered in flour and dough.

"You want to talk about Tommy?" she said, her elbows on the table, picking the dough from her hands.

I nodded.

"Why?"

I wasn't sure what to say and fumbled with my words.

She looked at the ring on my finger and my protruding belly. "Is the baby his?"

I nodded.

She took a deep breath and leaned back, crossing her arms over her chest. "How well do you know him?"

"I'm afraid not very well. I was hoping you could help me."

She shook her head. "I don't think you're going to like what I tell you."

I swallowed. "Okay."

She unfolded her arms and put a hand on her cheek. When she pulled it away, the flour remained. "Tommy grew up here, just down the road a few houses. His mother was my sister-in-law by marriage. I married one brother; she married the other. She died when Tommy was young. I wish she had lived; Tommy needed a mother." She sat forward and placed her elbows back on the table. "His father was...," she shook her head, "mean. He was always beating one of the kids. He drank a lot, and Tommy, being the oldest, got the brunt of it." She held up her hand. "Now, mind you, Tommy was no angel. The kid was a little piece of hell. He was always getting into trouble and never obeyed the rules. I have four kids myself, and Tommy was hanging around my youngest a lot. He wasn't a good influence. I tried to be patient with him, but the older he got, the more I could see my Jimmy had to stay away from him. He was always stealing something or chasing girls. The Morgan girl in town liked him. The two of them ran off together and got married. They were living in Denver until she turned up dead."

"Dead?"

She nodded; a grave look on her face. "Her body was found in a field. From the sounds of it, it wasn't a pretty picture. Her body had been there for months. It took them a while to figure out who she was. Tommy was long gone and hasn't been seen around these parts since."

She stood from the table and held up a finger, then walked to the oven. She opened the door while I sat, trying to absorb what she had told me. She opened the door fully, and I could see the bread pan with a lovely, golden-brown loaf protruding from the top. She pulled it out, closed the door, and tipped the bread over on the counter. The loaf dropped from the pan with a "plop," and she turned it over with her bare hand. She rubbed the hand on her apron, then blew on it. She turned off the oven, then came and sat back down.

"Where is he now?"

"Austin, Texas."

She looked at me strangely. "You don't sound Texan."

"I'm not. I'm from Chicago."

She nodded. "That sounds right. How did you meet him?"

"He came to Chicago, calling himself Charles Watson. He was looking for a loan from my father."

"And you fell for him."

I looked down and nodded.

She reached over and patted my hand. "Oh, don't feel bad. You aren't the only one. He has that effect on young girls. And he married you?"

"Yes."

"How long ago?"

"Just a few months."

"You were pregnant?"

I looked down again and nodded.

She leaned back and sighed, crossing her arms. "How did you find me?"

"He had a picture. His name was on the back, and it said Colorado Springs. He was just a boy in the picture, but I could tell it was him. The names on the back were Robert and Thomas Slater."

"That was his father and him."

She stood from the table and went to the counter. She placed the bread on a cutting board and began slicing it. I marveled at the expertise. I'd tried making bread several times, and it never turned out like hers. She placed two slices on a plate and brought them over with bread and jam.

"Do you like raspberry jam?"

I nodded.

She covered one slice with butter, then spread thick, red jam over the top. She handed it to me, and I thanked her. The smell was wonderful, but I wasn't sure I could eat it. What she had told me made me sick.

"Take a bite. You'll be all right."

I nodded and took a small bite. It was delicious. Nothing like homemade bread.

"Barbara," she said, looking into my eyes. "Now, listen to me, child. Promise me you won't go back to him. Promise me you'll go back to Chicago, to your family. Promise me you'll stay far away from Tommy."

She stared at me, and I didn't hesitate. "I promise."

Chapter 30

Louise

After Aunt Bea and I finished our bread, she called her husband in from the field and asked him to give me a lift back to town. I was surprised when he didn't ask who I was or where I had come from. Instead, he brought his buggy around to the front of the house. Before I stepped off the porch, I felt Aunt Bea's hand on my shoulder. She turned me around to look at her.

"Barbara, go home. Go back to Chicago. Tell your parents about Tommy. Talk to the police. You don't have to do this alone; do you hear me?"

I looked up into her face and nodded, then stepped off the porch and walked to the buggy. For ten minutes, we rode along silently. Aunt Bea's husband, Tommy's uncle, didn't say a word, which was fine with me. I wasn't in the mood to talk. How are you supposed to react when you learn your husband is, without a doubt, a murderer? Are you supposed to cry? Wail uncontrollably? I wondered what Aunt Bea thought of me. Did I react the way she would have wanted? Did the silent man sitting next to me know?

In all the books I'd read, I had never come across one titled, *So You've Married a Murderer. Now What?* Even that title wouldn't accurately show my situation. If only it were that easy. For my book, you'd have to add a line to the title. It'd be something like, *So You've Married a Murderer and You're About to Have His Baby: A How-To Guide.*

We reached town, and my driver finally spoke.

"Is this the spot?"

I nodded, and he pulled up in front. He helped me down, and I entered the hotel, passing several patrons as I walked through the foyer. I nearly bumped into one gentleman. He was a massive man with a long beard and an animal-skinned jacket. He looked like he'd be more comfortable spending the night in a teepee than in a hotel. I climbed the stairs to the second floor, reached my room, and fumbled with the key. My hands were shaking as I tried to fit the key in the lock, and I had difficulty shoving it in the hole. I stopped, took a few deep breaths, then tried again. The key turned, and the door opened. I stepped inside the room and closed the door behind me. I collapsed on the bed, forgetting how uncomfortable it felt to lie on my belly. As I turned over, I saw a man standing over me.

"Richard?"

His hand clamped over my mouth. "This doesn't look like Chicago, Louise."

Chapter 31

Louise

I opened my eyes as I heard horse hooves shuffle to a stop outside the dank cabin I'd been sleeping in. Sunlight streamed through the uneven boards that acted as walls in the shelter Richard had put me in. After surprising me in the hotel last night, he taped my mouth and bound my hands and feet at the wrists and ankles. He left me lying on the bed as he sat in a chair opposite me. We glared at each other for hours, neither speaking, until he finally stood and left the room, locking the door behind himself. After several minutes, I rolled to the edge of the bed and considered my options. I knew I could roll off, but decided against it. Bound as I was, with my arms behind my back, I wouldn't be able to catch myself and would likely land on my stomach, injuring the baby. Eventually, I gave up and rolled back to the middle of the bed and prayed. I asked God to send someone to the room. I begged him to save me. But he didn't.

An hour later, long after the sun had gone down, Richard returned. He walked to the bed, and I cowered away from him, afraid of what he might do. He held a knife and pointed it at me. I held my breath as he lowered it from my chest to the ropes that bound my legs. After freeing me, he grabbed my shoulders and pulled me to the edge of the bed, then helped me stand. I stood before him, petrified and uncertain. He looked down at me, and for the first time in hours, he spoke. The words were low and sharp.

"We're leaving. Louise, I don't want to hurt you. But I will if you force me."

I believed him. He had killed a wife before. He held up the knife, the light beaming off the tip. He waited, staring down at me, looking for an answer. I didn't hear a question, but I nodded. He grabbed my arm, moving me to the door. He opened it, poked his head around the corner, then pushed me out, the knife pressed against my back. I could feel the tip threatening to cut me. He walked behind me as I descended the stairs, his large hand wrapped around my bicep. I considered trying to break loose, making a run for it, but I knew it was futile. He was bigger, stronger, and faster. Even if I weren't pregnant, I'd be no match for him. He could do what he wanted to me, and I'd be powerless to stop him. My lip trembled below the tape at the thought.

When we reached the main floor, I looked at the registration desk with hope, but saw it was unoccupied. It must have been at least two a.m., and everyone except us was asleep. We exited through the side door to a waiting horse and buggy. I turned to look at him, but he just pushed me toward the stairs leading to the seat. He joined me, snapping the reins and guiding the coach through the deserted streets.

Before long, we were outside of town, gliding along the dirt path. The only sound was the clip-clop of hooves as we moved further into the country. His cold, emotionless demeanor scared me more than anything. I would have preferred he scream and yell and hit me.

After what must have been thirty minutes, he turned off the road and followed an overgrown path to a small wooden cabin near a creek. The area was dark, other than the bright, full moon. At the cabin, he stopped and pulled me with him as he descended the steps. He pushed me toward the structure, and that's when I started to fight. I turned and kicked him, then struggled to get free. I did all I could to break loose of his grip, but he was too strong.

He dragged me toward the structure with no doors or windows. I knew I was going to my death. He had killed before, maybe more than once. The setting was eerily similar to his first wife. He had left her body in a shallow grave in a field in Colorado. I imagined he would take me inside, kill me, then either leave my body until the grave was dug or skip town. It could be days or weeks before anyone would find me, if they ever did.

Once inside, the roof of the structure blocked the moonlight, and my heart beat so fast I thought it might pound out of my chest. I wondered how he might do it—a slice to the neck or a blade to my heart. I wondered if it would hurt, or if it would be so quick that the pain wouldn't register before I stopped breathing.

I stood, waiting, anticipating the blade, but it never came. Instead, he led me to a corner and began rebinding my legs. I was over allowing him to mistreat me and kicked my feet. I struck him, and he cursed before gripping my leg and punching my quad muscle right above the knee. The pain was so sharp it made me gasp and cry out. I fell back against the wall, crumpling to the ground. He grabbed my legs again, sitting on my feet, and finished tying them at the ankles. The fight was out of me.

He stood, and I listened in the dark to his footsteps moving away. His shadow filled the door frame, and I thought he might say something, but he just turned and walked out. Moments later, I heard him climb aboard the buggy and drive away, leaving me alone in the dark, dusty cabin with packed-dirt floors, gasping in pain from the punch to my leg and the tightness of the ropes around my ankles and wrists.

With my back against the cabin wall, my thoughts went to what might become of me. I wondered if any animals might be in these woods. If a pack of wolves might circle the structure, their howls growing louder as they closed in. Before long, I stopped worrying about what might come from outside the cabin to what was already with me. I imagined spiders crawling up my dress. Snakes and rats eager to sample human flesh.

Eventually, exhaustion overcame my fears. I gave up worrying, shifted my weight to reduce the pressure on my bound arms, and drifted off. When I woke, it was morning, and someone was outside. I assumed it was him, but allowed myself to hope that it could be someone else. Maybe they saw the tracks and came to investigate. I heard footsteps approach the cabin, and when I saw who it was, the disappointment was so sharp I could almost taste it. Richard filled the doorframe of the cabin. Our eyes met, and I rolled from my side to my back. Dried grass and dirt covered one side of my face. He approached, and I cowered in fear as he extended his hand. I expected pain, violence, but he brushed the dirt from my cheek and chin and picked the grass from my hair. Fear gave way to curiosity and surprise. I no longer saw the same anger as the night before.

He reached for the tape over my mouth and pulled at the edges. I flinched, and he watched me before ripping down in a lightning motion. My lips erupted in pain, and I could feel myself breathing hard as he supported my back and helped me to lean against the wall. Once I was settled, my arms and legs still bound, I noticed he had water and food. He had left it on the floor when he came in and now went back to retrieve it. He poured the water into a cup, then held it to my lips. I savored the taste, not realizing how thirsty I'd become. After I drained the cup, he pulled it back and sat on the floor a few feet away from me.

"Better?"

I didn't trust myself to speak, and nodded.

He watched me, his blue eyes dark and hooded. "I have some questions I want to ask, and I don't want any lies. I want honesty." Hate filled my eyes. "Okay?"

"No."

"No? Louise, you're not in the position to negotiate."

"You want answers from me?"

He nodded.

"Untie my hands and feet."

He shook his head.

"What? Are you afraid of me?"

He chuckled, shaking his head. "Hardly. I just don't want to chase you when you run. Plus, you have the baby to think of."

With one word, he had crystallized why I was still alive. Why he was feeding me. I carried his baby, and that's what he wanted. I was only useful to him until the baby was born. Strange as that might sound, it was a comfort. I had time.

"At least untie my arms. I still won't be able to run with my legs bound."

He raised an eyebrow, considering it. Shrugging, he came forward. I moved to the side so he could access the rope at my hands. After a few seconds, I felt the release of pressure at my wrists as he pulled away the rope. The fronts of my shoulders were sore as I brought my arms forward. They'd been locked in the same position for so long, they were numb. He returned to his spot on the floor opposite me, and I placed my hands on my knees.

"How did you know to come here?"

I stared back at him, considering my options. I knew I could never trust him again, but I also had to be smart. I needed to play his game and wait for the right moment to strike.

"I found a picture of you with your father. On the back, it had your name and Colorado Springs."

He nodded. "What did Aunt Bea tell you?"

"That you murdered your wife."

His eyes didn't even blink. He gave no reaction. "And you believe her?"

I shook my head. "I don't know what to believe. I hope it's not true. I can't imagine you doing that."

He continued to watch me closely. "I didn't. She was sick, not physically. It was in her head. She changed. All she wanted, all she cared about, was having a baby. For months, we tried, but she couldn't get pregnant. She couldn't handle it. Depression overcame her. She blamed me. She was angry with me, with her life. I didn't realize how bad it was until one day I came home. She had cut her own throat. Blood covered the floor. It was awful. When I approached her lifeless body, I found bruises covering her. She had beaten herself with the iron rod we kept next to the fire. I realized then that her hate for me was complete. It wasn't enough that she killed herself, she wanted me to suffer. She wanted me to be blamed."

"What did you do?"

He shook his head. "The only thing I could think to do. Bury the evidence. I loaded her into the back of a wagon and drove her to a secluded field. I dug a hole and left her there, hoping nobody would find her."

"Well, they did."

"Is that what Aunt Bea said?"

I nodded.

"Believe me, Louise. I did nothing wrong. I know I should have gone to the police and told them what had happened, but they wouldn't have believed me, and I was scared. I couldn't take that chance."

"I believe you."

He sighed in relief.

"But why didn't you tell me this before? Why so many secrets?"

He shrugged. "I'm sorry. I should have. I just...she hurt me so badly. It's hard for me to trust another woman."

He came toward me and untied my legs. I stretched them, moving them back and forth, happy that I had fooled him.

"Are you hungry?"

I nodded. He handed me an apple, and I bit into it. Juice ran down my chin, and I wiped it away with the back of my hand. "Let's go home," I said.

He agreed and helped me to my feet. He picked up the food, and we walked out to the buggy. Once we were seated and headed back to the road, I rummaged through the bag and pulled out a slice of bread. As I brought it to my mouth, I stopped. I recognized the smell. Before that moment, bread had always seemed so common, so usual, that I wouldn't consider its scent. Although it smelled good, I couldn't smell the difference between one recipe and another. I thought it was all the same. That's when I realized I was wrong. Different bakers used different ingredients. No two loaves were the same. Every loaf had its unique smell, its unique flavor. This was the same bread I had smelled yesterday. The same bread I had tasted fresh from the oven.

I knew now where he had gone when he had left me last night. I could see it from the mud on his shoes and the dirt on his hands. He had eliminated loose ends. The only people who knew who I was and where he was living.

I took a bite of the bread and relaxed back on the seat. He smiled at me, and I smiled back. I turned and looked at the mountains in the distance, pretending to marvel at the scene. But my attention wasn't on the jagged peaks. My focus was on three months. I had three months to plan my escape. After that, I'd have done what he wanted, and he'd have no more use for me.

Chapter 32

Michael

Michael looks down at the note in his notepad, then back up at the two-story house nestled in the wealthy suburb of Chicago, called Oak Park. *This must be it*; he thinks. The street number on the house matches the note. He walks along the circular drive, up the stairs, and knocks on the door. Nobody answers, but before he knocks again, a middle-aged woman opens the inside door. They look at each other through the screen.

"Yes, can I help you?"

"Mrs. Clifford?"

The woman shakes her head. "No, Mrs. Clifford is resting inside. What's this about?"

"My name is Michael Delaney. I need to talk to her about her daughter."

"Barbara?"

"Yes."

"Has something happened?"

"I'm sorry, ma'am. I'd feel more comfortable talking with Mrs. Clifford directly."

The woman comes forward and opens the screen door for him. He can see from the tremble in her lip and the lines around her eyes, he's worried her.

"Come inside, please." She ushers him through the entrance, and his eyes are drawn to the staircase. He can't remember seeing anything like it. He imagines it might be something you'd find in the White House. "Wait here."

The woman, obviously the housekeeper, ascends the stairs and disappears while he stands gazing at the large chandelier hanging above his head. While he waits, he counts the number of lights. Although electricity isn't new, it isn't cheap, and he wonders about the cost of running a light like this. Not to mention how tall the ladder must be to replace each bulb.

The housekeeper returns, walking toward him down the stairs. "Mrs. Clifford will see you in the library."

She leads him down a hallway, then stops beside the fourth door on the left. She opens the door, and light fills the room. A large window sits on the opposite wall, the drapes open, allowing daylight to flood the room. A solid, round table sits in the middle of the space. On either wall, floor-to-ceiling bookcases house hundreds of books.

The woman points to a chair around the table. "Please, sit. She'll be with you shortly."

Michael does as he's told, and the housekeeper leaves the room. He squints at the bookcases, trying to read some titles on the spines of the books.

The door reopens, and Michael stands as Mrs. Clifford enters the room. He guesses she's in her mid to late forties. Her hair is light with gray mixed throughout. She's thin with a delicate curve to her body. She's a beautiful woman now. He can only imagine what she looked like twenty years ago. She has impeccable posture, and if he knew anything about clothing, he'd guess her attire was expensive.

"Mr. Delaney?"

"Yes, ma'am."

"Please, sit back down."

He follows her command, and she walks to the other side of the table and sits. She looks at him, and he can see by the tremble in her hand, her housekeeper has warned her.

"Ma'am, I'm not here about Barbara."

Her eyebrows raise with surprise.

"I want to talk about your other daughter."

Mrs. Clifford takes a sharp breath. "Louise?"

So that's the name...

"Yes, ma'am."

"Have you found her? Where is she? Is she okay?"

Michael holds up a hand as she rises out of her seat. "Ma'am, I'm sorry. I don't know where Louise is. I was hoping you might help me locate her."

Mrs. Clifford sits back down dejectedly. "You don't know where she is?"

"No, I'm sorry."

She frowns, and even though she's half his size and older, her look frightens him. "Then what are you doing here asking me about her?"

"Ma'am, I'm trying to find her. I hoped you could tell me where she is."

A hardness enters her speech. "And what makes you think I know, Mr. Delaney? Who are you, and why are you looking for Louise?"

Michael tells her he's a detective from Denver. That he's been tracking a man named Thomas Slater of Colorado Springs. He tells her about finding him in a jail in Kansas City. About learning of his other identities, Ernest Johns, Richard Amhurst, and Charles Watson. She nearly jumps out of her chair at the last name.

"Charles?"

"Yes, ma'am."

"He's in Kansas City? Not Houston?"

"That's correct."

"And Louise, was she with him?"

Michael hesitates. "It appears she might have been. In Austin."

"Texas?"

"Yes, ma'am." Michael pauses, unsure of how to say the next part. "Ma'am, it looks as if she married him. She was pregnant with his child."

Mrs. Clifford looks away. "I know," she whispers.

"You know?"

Mrs. Clifford exhales a slow breath and doesn't meet his eyes. "That's why she left here. It's why she chased after him. I knew she was pregnant. I can recognize the signs."

"Forgive me, ma'am. You knew she went after him?"

Mrs. Clifford looks up. Her green eyes sparkle, and Michael is taken aback by her beauty. "We went to New York City for a family funeral. My sister and her husband died unexpectedly. Charles went with us. He was a business acquaintance of my husband's. When we came back, he stayed in New York. I could tell by Louise's reaction that something was going on between them. I took my time confronting her. She could be difficult." Mrs. Clifford shakes her head. "Not long after our return, she snuck away one night. We hired an investigator to find her, but he made it to Houston and no further."

Michael can see the pain in her eyes. "Ma'am, I'm afraid the news isn't good."

Mrs. Clifford stops breathing, her eyes fixed on him.

"She hasn't been seen since Austin. Charles, as you know him, fled Austin to Kansas City, and Louise wasn't with him. The marshal of Austin believes Charles killed her, and I'm afraid I do too. You see, Charles has killed before. More than once."

Mrs. Clifford sits in her chair perfectly still, her green eyes burning a hole through him. Finally, a shake of her head. "No, I won't accept that. Call it a mother's intuition, Mr. Delaney, but she's not dead. I feel it in my heart. She's alive."

Michael sees the same heartache he saw two years ago at the bedside of another mother whose daughter was a victim of Thomas Slater. That one didn't work out, and he's afraid this one won't have a happy ending either.

Chapter 33

Louise

I laid on our bed, my dress hiked up to my waist, as the doctor examined me. He'd been there every week since we'd returned, and every week Richard was there too.

I raised my arm to look at my watch. I knew what time it was, but I hoped that maybe by looking at the watch I'd time warp five or ten minutes into the future and this would be over. As I examined my arm, it was my skin, not the watch, that captured my attention. I'd always been fair-skinned, never one to tan well, but what little tint of brown I had from my park chats with Mary and my attempted escape to Colorado Springs was gone.

We had returned to Austin a month ago, and I hadn't been allowed to leave the house. Upon our return, right when we had walked into the house, Richard sat me down at the kitchen table. He told me he had to punish me for what I had done. A wife was to obey her husband, and I had displeased him. I had broken his trust, and I would have to earn it back. Then he doled out his sentence. I wouldn't be permitted to leave the house until after the baby was born. Anything I needed; he would bring for me. He also told me visitors weren't allowed. If someone came and rang the bell, I was to ignore it. If I obeyed, after the baby was born, I would earn back the right to venture out occasionally.

That night, after he fell asleep, I considered sneaking away. I wanted to run, get as far away from him as possible. Lying in bed next to him was almost more than I could bear. I almost did it, but I knew better. I'd never been a patient person. I'd always acted on impulse. That's how I got there, pregnant and married to him.

I couldn't repeat the past. I knew for me to escape; I had to be patient. I had to plan.

"You can sit up now, Barbara," the doctor said and offered me his hand, pulling me to a sitting position.

I pulled down my dress and sat with my legs hanging off the bed. My arms were behind my back, supporting my ever-increasing weight.

"How are your headaches?" he asked, watching me closely.

I stole a glance at Richard before answering. "Better."

I began to squirm under his penetrating gaze.

"Good. Maybe you can get outside then. Resume your walks. Walking is very important for the baby and you."

I glanced at Richard, then back to the doctor. "Actually, I think it's the sun that gives me the headaches. It's been much better when I've stayed inside."

"Oh?"

"Yes...just yesterday I tried to go out, but two minutes in the sun, and the headaches came back."

The doctor frowned and watched me even more closely.

"But you said the headaches have been better."

I looked at Charles and moved to answer, but he cut me off, taking a step toward the doctor. "What I think my wife is trying to say is that she's noticed when she stays out of the sun, her headaches are better. Lately, she's been staying inside, and things have been much better. Yesterday, she tried again, wanting to follow your directions, but the headaches came back."

The doctor turned in his chair to look at Charles, then back at me. He made a note in his notepad. "I see." He finished writing and looked back up, speaking to me. "You know how I feel about you walking. Like we talked about before when you complained about the heat, there's nothing wrong with walking at night. I'd prefer you get some sun, but if that's not possible, at least walks at night. You need the exercise. Perhaps Mr. Amhurst could accompany you." He turned and looked at Richard, and Richard nodded. "Good."

The doctor stood and prepared to leave the room when Richard said, "Doctor, how long until she has the baby? How are things looking?"

The doctor's response quickened my pulse.

"I should think a baby will be here in two to three weeks. Things are progressing nicely."

"Can you tell the sex yet?"

The doctor chuckled and shook his head. "I'm not that kind of doctor. You'd need to go to New Orleans for that type of medicine. Just hold tight to your wallet while you're there."

The doctor smiled and nodded to me, and Charles walked him out of the room. I heard them talking in low voices, but couldn't make out the words. Finally, I heard the front door open and shut. Moments later, Richard returned.

"Good news," Richard said, leaning against the door frame to our bedroom. "Less than a month and you'll be able to deliver. I'm sure you're eager to be free of the extra weight."

"Yes, it's very exciting," I said, forcing a smile.

He moved toward me, and I reminded myself to welcome his embrace. He put his arms around me, and I rested my head against his stomach, grateful I didn't have to look into his eyes, worrying they would betray me.

"I know you're scared, but your doctor is the best in the state. You're in expert hands."

I nodded without looking at him. He kissed the top of my head, then stepped away. He moved to leave the room, but paused midway.

"I have to go to the hotel for a while. Let's not have a repeat of yesterday."

He stood still, his back to me, waiting for an answer, but I said nothing. He left the room, and I remained seated on the bed, listening to his movements in the kitchen. Finally, he opened and shut the front door, and he was gone. I stood and went to the window. I looked out in time to see him reach the street. He looked to his left, and I saw what, or who, he was looking for. A man stood in the pecan tree's shadow, two houses down. I couldn't tell for sure, but I thought it was the same man I had seen yesterday. I turned away from the window and walked back to the bed. I picked up my pillow, pressed it to my face, and screamed.

After a few minutes, I walked down the hall to the front room. I picked up my book, but I couldn't focus on the words. I was a prisoner in my own house. These were my last several days, and they'd be spent trapped, locked away.

Yesterday, I had defied Richard and left the house. I went to the park and sat on the bench, hoping to see Mary. I wasn't there fifteen minutes before Richard walked into the park and sat down next to me. Behind him, in the shadow of another tree, I noticed a man watching us. He had followed me from the house and notified Richard.

Richard had walked me back to the house, saying nothing. Once inside, he took me to the bathroom and made me sit in the tub. He tied my legs and arms together, just like he had in Colorado Springs. He told me he was disappointed in me, put a cup of water on the ledge, and left. There I sat, for hours, powerless to move. Staring at the bathroom wall with nothing else to occupy my mind.

With the growth of the baby, my bladder had shrunk. Within an hour, I peed myself. I realized that's why he had left me in the tub. When he returned home, I begged him to remove the restraints. I promised to never leave again, and he gave me one more chance. He removed them and let me bathe and clean up. He fed me dinner, then we went to bed. As I lay there, listening to him breathe, I considered how I might kill him. But again, I restrained myself. The time hadn't come.

A knock at the front door brought my attention away from the words on the page I wasn't reading. I tiptoed to the window and looked out. My friend, Mary Tuberville, stood on the porch. Her back was to the door, looking out at the street. I looked toward the pecan tree and saw the man standing there, watching. Mary turned back to the door and knocked again, louder this time. I stood motionless, watching her. She pulled at the door, but it was locked. Finally, she gave up and walked down the steps and out onto the path to the street. She walked around the corner and was gone. I breathed a sigh of relief. I would have loved to have spent time with her, to have told her what was going on with me, but with the man watching the house, I knew I couldn't.

I went to the kitchen and cut myself several slices of cheese from the block in the ice chest, placed them on a plate, and sat down at the kitchen table. Before long, I heard a dog barking at a house behind mine and saw Mary climbing the neighbor's fence, her dress pulled up to her waist, her petticoat open to the world. She jumped down, crossed the grass behind our house, and reached the back door. It was unlocked, and she didn't bother to knock. She came exploding into the room like she owned the place. Our eyes locked. I was seated at the kitchen table. She closed the door behind her and sat down in Richard's chair across from me.

"You don't look sick. What's going on?" she said, pulling the plate of cheese from me and picking up a slice. She popped it in her mouth, then gave me a look like *I'm waiting*. I was so shocked I couldn't speak. I just stared at her. "Well?"

"Who told you I was sick?"

"Richard. Who do you think?"

I felt a lurch of fear. "When did you talk to him? Does he know you're here?"

"No. He said you were sick in bed. That the doctor has been with you. That you can't have any visitors. You don't look sick to me. What's going on?"

I stood from the table and went to the back door and opened it.

"You have to leave."

She sat at the table, ignoring me.

"I'm serious."

Finally, she looked at me. "Not until you tell me why you're avoiding me. Did I do something to make you mad?"

I closed the door and sat back down across from her. "It's not anything like that."

"Then what is it?"

"You wouldn't believe me if I told you."

"Is it Richard?"

I stole a glance behind me, worried somehow he'd be there. He'd know.

Her eyes went wide. "It is Richard. What's he doing?"

"You remember what you told me about the girl who went to Dallas? The one who ran away."

"Yeah."

"I don't think she ran away."

"What? What do you mean?"

I told her everything. I told her about finding the picture and going to Colorado Springs. About him finding me and tying me up. About coming home and being forbidden to leave the house. I told her about what he had done to me yesterday. Through the whole thing, she watched me, barely blinking. When I finished, she slapped her hand on the table. It made me jump.

"We've got to get you out of here."

She stood and came around the table, gripping my arm, but I pulled away.

"No."

"What? Why not?"

"There's a man out there."

"What man?"

"A man under the pecan tree in the front."

She walked to the front room and then came back several seconds later.

"I can't leave. Richard will find me."

"He's going to kill you."

I shook my head. "Not as long as I'm pregnant with his baby."

She sat back down. "How long do you have?"

"Two or three weeks. A month, at most."

"No, you don't."

"That's what the doctor said today."

"Yeah, but what if he's wrong? What if you go into labor early? And even then, how are you going to escape with a baby in your arms? Barbara, you have to tell someone. Let me do it. Let me go to the sheriff."

"And say what? Look at me. Do I look like I've been abused? There's hardly a mark on me. No way a man is going to believe me over Richard. He's so charismatic, you've seen him. The sheriff will end up arresting me."

She knows I'm right. It's a man's world we live in.

She sits back in the chair, a finger tapping her lips.

"What are you going to do?"

"I've got a plan, and you could help."

Chapter 34

Louise

It had been a week since Mary snuck into the house, and she had been back every day since. At the time, I didn't want her to come. I didn't want to involve anyone in my problems, and I knew just how dangerous Richard could be. Obviously, I worried about her safety, but it wasn't just that. I imagined him finding out and punishing me. To that point, thankfully, he seemed to have no idea. In fact, things had been better between us. I played the part of the obedient wife who only wanted her husband's love, staying inside and eating my vegetables like the doctor wanted.

Any time Richard touched me, my skin crawled. I loathed him. My hate for him fueled my escape plans, which were progressing nicely. Since Mary had come back into my life, I felt like I had a chance. I couldn't have done it without her. She had resources and freedom that were invaluable to me. Every day we'd bounce ideas off each other, and her connections gave me confidence. Today was to be our final meeting, and tonight I would put our plan in place. Now, I was waiting for her to arrive.

I looked at my watch and noticed the time. She should have been there at any moment. I struggled my way to the end of the couch and pushed off the arm to stand. My book slid off the couch and toppled to the floor. I cursed under my breath. It had become an effort to walk, but picking something up off the floor? Forget about it. I stood looking down at it, hands on my hips. I planned to take it with me to the kitchen. I could read it until Mary arrived, but now I didn't think it was worth the effort. Shaking my head with frustration, I left it on the floor and waddled to the kitchen table. I sat down and stared out the window, waiting for Mary.

After several minutes of staring, lost in thought, I looked down at my watch. She was late. She'd never been late before. Which I found surprising. She was such a free spirit; I would have thought time wouldn't matter to her, but it did. I felt a rush of concern but tried to pass it off. Maybe she got caught up. Perhaps our final preparations were taking longer than we had expected. Maybe she had hit a snag. I sat, staring out the back window, waiting for her to pop up over the fence, her dress snagging on the wooden planks.

After ten more minutes, my concern morphed into panic. I stood away from the table and looked out the window. I saw no evidence of her. I turned around and walked down the hallway to our bedroom. I approached the window and looked out. What I saw surprised me. The man was gone for the first time since we had returned from Colorado Springs.

I walked back to the front room and looked out that window, thinking maybe he was less obvious now. I searched the street, looking in every possible spot. Nothing, nobody. An occasional person walked past or a man riding horseback, but nobody was watching the house. I looked at the book on the floor and shuffled over to it. I squatted down and reached until I could get enough of my hand on it to pick it up. As I stood, I exhaled, not realizing I was holding my breath. I waddled back to the kitchen, sat down at the table, and opened the book. I read the words, but my mind continued to wander. Where was Mary? And where was the man Richard had watching the house?

A noise behind me brought my head around, and I turned to see Richard entering the front door. He looked to the back of the house and saw me sitting at the table. He carried a sack in his hand. Seeing me, he waved, shutting the door behind him. A surge of alarm raced through me. What was he doing home? What if Mary came? I moved to get up from the table, but he'd already reached the kitchen before I could stand.

"Don't get up." He placed the sack on the counter. "I thought I'd come home and bring you lunch today. From the sounds of it, we won't be able to do this much longer."

I wondered what that meant, but smiled and said, "How wonderful."

He looked at the book in my hand. "Wow, that's a big book. What's it called?"

I turned it over so he could see the cover.

"*A Tale of Two Cities* by Charles Dickens," he read aloud, then turned away and got two plates from the cabinet. "Is it any good?"

"Yes, very."

"What's it about?"

I looked out the window, worrying I'd see Mary dangling on the top. "Well, most people would say it's about the French Revolution. But I'd say it's a love story that just happens to take place during the revolution."

He was preparing sandwiches for us and not looking at me. I stood and walked over to the back door, looking out.

"Does she end up with her man?"

"Who?"

"The woman in the book. I assume, if it's a love story, there must be some man she loves."

He finished with the sandwiches and brought them to the table. He walked back to the ice chest, poured us both large cups of milk, and set them on the table. I supported myself on the table and leaned down to the chair. He saw me struggling, set down the cups, and helped me. I stole another glance at the back of the house. He saw me and turned to look.

"You won't see her," he said, turning back around. His eyes were like ice.

"What?"

"Mary. Don't bother looking."

I felt my jaw drop and my mouth open. We stared at each other across the table, the sandwiches between us. His face was relaxed, emotionless. It was as if he had said a very common thing, nothing to think about.

"In fact, she won't be visiting again. Ever."

"What are you talking about?"

He grimaced. "Louise, I know you think I'm a fool. Someone you can manipulate. But I'm way ahead of you. I know she's been visiting you for a week. I know what you've been planning." He takes a big bite of his chicken sandwich and looks at me. "Eat up. You need your strength. That baby's going to be here soon."

Chapter 35

Louise

The water was chilly, and it covered every inch of my body, except my face. I was flat on my back, looking up at the ceiling. When I first dipped a toe in the bathwater, I wondered if it would scald me. It was so hot that I had to wait a few minutes before getting in. That was an hour before, and my teeth chattered. I raised one hand above the water and looked at my fingers. The skin was wrinkled. They looked like the hands of a woman twice my age. I knew if I stayed in the water much longer, I could develop hypothermia. Much longer than that, and I could die. It was a welcome thought. If I killed myself, it'd remove the pleasure from Richard. I knew he was just outside the door. He'd never let me do it, anyway. He wanted the baby.

A sharp pain emanated from my gut, and I forced myself to take long, slow breaths. I pushed down the panic that rose inside me. More and more frequently, I'd been experiencing labor pains. Each time, I could breathe my way through them, but I knew eventually they'd be for real. The contractions would continue, and I wouldn't be able to stop them. I'd be giving life to another being while ending my own.

The baby moved, and I felt it kick. How was it possible that I could carry another life inside me yet feel hollow? As if I had nothing left to live for. Richard had won. He'd done something to Mary and foiled my plans. I didn't know how, but he knew what I was going to do.

I looked down at my overgrown stomach and the recent development. I'd always had an inverted belly button. It was like a hole in the middle of my stomach. I used to lie in bed at night, putting my finger in it and daydreaming of falling in love. *Both are impossible*, I thought. My belly button stuck out like a new nose growing from my stomach. And love? I reached down and brushed my hand over the nose.

The thought brought a wave of emotion, and tears spilled out of my eyes and slid into the water. The nose I would never see. I'd carried the baby for nearly nine months, yet I'd never be able to raise it. Was it a girl? Would she look like me? Maybe she'd take after her aunt, the real Barbara. Maybe a cross between my sister and husband. Barbara's lean, trim figure and Richard's bright-blue eyes. How lovely she would be.

Or maybe a boy. A boy would have been nice. Tall like my father, with Richard's piercing eyes and granite chin. But would he become like Richard? A monster?

My eyes returned to my belly, and I wondered about the spirit inside. I thought about Richard's father. He had beaten him. Would Richard do the same? Create a hard, psychopathic man? Someone incapable of feeling empathy?

I gritted my chattering teeth. No, I wouldn't allow it. He would not have my child.

I pushed up out of the water and stood from the tub, being careful about my foot placement. I reached for the towel and dried myself before walking to the sink and the mirror above it. I looked in the mirror at my reflection and barely recognized the eyes that looked back at me. If my plan didn't work, I knew I had to kill myself. I wouldn't let him raise my child.

I look behind me at the thick scab on the back of my thigh. A week ago, I had cut myself deep enough to draw blood and squeezed blood into a jar like a farmer milked a cow. I stored it in the back of the cupboard here in the bathroom. Somewhere Richard wouldn't look. I opened the cabinet door and moved products out of the way until I reached it. I removed the lid and poured the contents onto the bathroom floor. Thick, dark blood covered the ground. To make the story more believable, I dipped my fingers into the jar and wiped the blood between my legs. I turned on the water and rinsed out the jar, removing all remnants of the blood that had been stored in it.

I scanned the room, making sure I hadn't forgotten anything. When I was certain, I looked in the mirror and contorted my face. I screamed, gasped for breath, and screamed again. Seconds later, the door opened, with Richard standing in the doorframe, looking at me. I looked up from my hunched-over position, torment in my eyes. He looked down and saw the blood covering the floor.

"What..." He looked up at me. "Louise?"

"I don't know," I said, then screamed again. I pretended to falter, and he grabbed my outstretched hand. "Help me," I begged.

His face was white with panic. "Let's get you to the bed."

He wrapped a hand around my waist and supported me as I walked hunched over to our bedroom. When I reached the bed, I placed a hand on the mattress and screamed again, sobbing. He let me go, turning to leave the room.

"I'll call the doctor."

He left the room, and I supported my weight and pushed up on the bed, lying flat with a towel covering me. After several seconds, I screamed again and worked up more tears. After a few minutes, he came back into the room. He stood over the bed, eyeing me. To sell the emergency, I thrashed back and forth, exposing my lower half. I saw him look and notice the blood. The skepticism I saw in his eyes was gone now. He believed something was wrong.

Gasping for breath, I asked, "Doctor?"

He came forward but didn't touch me. "He's coming. He'll be here soon."

Over the next several minutes, I cried out in pain, over and over, while sobbing. I was quite the actress. Maybe it was all the productions my mother had taken me to as a little girl.

Finally, I heard the front door open, and Richard rushed out of the room.

"In here?" he called.

The doctor entered carrying a medical bag. He came to the bedside and looked down at me.

"What is it, Barbara? What happened?"

I gasped in pain and fought for breath. "I don't know. So much pain. Blood."
"Where?"

"In the bathroom," Richard said, standing beside the doctor.

"Show me," the doctor said, and Richard took him out of the room to the bathroom. Seconds later, he was back at the bedside. "We have to get you to a hospital, immediately."

"No," Richard said. "No hospitals."

The doctor turned and grabbed Richard by the shirt collar. "If we don't get your wife to the hospital right away, she'll die. Do you understand me?"

"No hospitals," Richard said.

The doctor shouted in his face. "Your wife and baby will die! Is that what you want?"

Richard stared back at him. Finally, he nodded.

The doctor released him and turned back to me.

"Barbara, can you stand?"

"I don't know," I said, breathlessly.

"Can you try?"

I nodded, and he helped me up, the towel dropping off of me. He saw the blood on my legs and put his arm around me.

"Get a blanket," he told Richard.

Richard sprung to the closet, brought back a blanket, and they wrapped it around me.

Once I was wrapped up like a mummy, the doctor instructed Richard to hold my legs while he took me by the shoulders. They laid me back and carried me from the house. When we reached the doctor's horse and buggy, they lifted me to the seat and placed me on it. My legs hung over the edge while the doctor crossed to the other side and sprang up, grabbing the reins.

"Can you rest your head on my lap?" he asked.

I raised my head, and he sat. I crashed back down, my head on his thighs. He called out to Richard, "Follow us."

Richard rushed to his horse as the doctor snapped the reins.

Chapter 36

Louise

We pulled up to the two-story brick building that served as the city hospital, and the doctor asked me to raise my head so he could stand. I leaned up on an elbow, and he stepped around me, jumped down from the buggy, and entered the hospital, leaving me to lie on the seat. Richard arrived right behind us, and rather than come to me, he tied up his horse and followed the doctor inside. I was left alone, lying on the seat with my elbow propped, watching.

After a couple of minutes, Richard, the doctor, and another man exited the hospital. They carried a small bed that looked more like a board with a sheet.

"Richard, go up and lift your wife by the shoulders. We'll hold the stretcher."

Richard circled the buggy and climbed up, taking me under the arms by the shoulders. I cried out in pain, begging for mercy. The doctor and the other man reached up and supported my legs. Then they carried me to the stretcher and placed me on it before lifting and bringing me into the hospital. Two nurses stood at the entrance. The doctor told the stouter one to take the other end of the stretcher from Richard. Richard released me, and the doctor motioned with his head to the other nurse.

I couldn't see him, because we'd moved past them, but I could hear her tell Richard he couldn't go any farther. He protested, and another nurse rushed past us toward the commotion as we moved down the hallway toward the back of the hospital. We crossed through a doorway and entered a room with a line of beds. Half of the beds were occupied. All the patients were women. Most had some type of injury. I saw bandages of every kind covering different areas of their bodies.

The doctor motioned with his head to the last bed, away from the other patients. They lifted me from the gurney and placed me on the bed. The nurse asked the doctor something, but I couldn't make out the words. I was still moaning and groaning, but not like I was around Richard.

"I want to talk to her for a few minutes," the doctor said. "Make sure the husband doesn't come back here."

She nodded and left. And it was just us. The other patients were too far away to hear our conversation.

"What's going on, Barbara?" He gave me a questioning stare.

"What do you mean?"

He pulled back the blanket, exposing my naked lower half.

"Look at that blood. It was dry by the time I reached the house. You aren't bleeding. You put it there. You seem perfectly fine to me. I went along because I was curious. Now, I want answers. You better have a good reason for putting us all in a panic tonight."

I pulled the blanket back and covered myself.

"I had to."

"Why?"

We stared at each other, and his next statement wasn't a question.

"Your husband."

I nodded. "After I have the baby, he's going to kill me."

"Kill you?" He looked skeptical.

I looked around the room. The other patients were watching us. Several nurses scurried around, but none were close enough to hear. I took no chances and lowered my voice.

"He was married before. He killed her in Colorado before he came here."

For several minutes, I told him all about Richard. Who he really was. Through the whole thing, he barely moved, watching me closely. When I finished, he opened his mouth to speak, but the nurse returned and cut him off.

"The husband is waiting in the front."

The doctor nodded and looked at me, then back at the nurse. "Carol, I can't tell you why, but this woman needs help. She needs to leave this hospital without being seen. Especially by her husband."

The nurse looked at me, then back at the doctor. "Is she able?"

"She'll be fine. Can you help her? I'm going to go keep the husband occupied. Take her out the back. Find her some clothes." He reached inside his pocket, withdrew a handful of dollar bills, and handed them to me. "Take this and get out of town. If what you say is true, he'll be coming for you."

Chapter 37

Louise

I whispered "goodbye" to Carol, the nurse, and stepped out the back door of the hospital. It was evening when we arrived, and now it was full dark. Carol had given me a dress to wear and some shoes, but neither fit well. I knew I shouldn't, but I had to go home. There was something there I needed for this plan to work. Plus, a pregnant woman with ill-fitting clothes would stick out like a sore thumb. Multiple people would remember me, and Richard would find them. The thought of returning shook me to no end, but I had to.

My anxiety was through the roof as I moved away from the building, walking down an alleyway. Visions of Richard coming around the corner danced through my mind, which only heightened the nauseous feeling I had. It was nearly ten p.m. on a Wednesday night, and the streets were quiet. I reached the end of the alleyway and stayed back in the shadows of the building, looking out at the street. I couldn't see anyone out, but the streetlight worried me. If Richard, or the man who worked for him, was near the front of the building and looked out, they could see me through the window. My heart felt like it was going to burst through my chest. Deciding I had no other choice, I stepped out of the shadows and crossed the street as quickly as my pregnant waddle would allow. When I reached the other side of the street, I ducked back into the shadows and walked along the walls of the locked stores.

I nearly tripped as I moved along the sidewalk, looking back every few steps. I was so worried I was being followed. It would be just like Richard to see me, trace my path, and then pounce when I'd reached a secluded spot.

I stopped to look around and catch my breath. I'd only lived in Austin for six months, and most of those months had seen me cooped up in the house, barely venturing out. I didn't know the city well, and I only had a vague sense of how to get home. I was on Brazos Street and knew I needed to exit. It was one of the busiest roads with plenty of light, and if Richard had left the hospital for home, it would be the route he would take. I cut down a side street and was greeted by a chorus of barking dogs. I prayed none of them were loose as I rumbled along.

I tripped on a tree limb and fell, but caught myself before striking my belly. Pain seared my palms and knees as the gravel from the road dug into my flesh. I stood and brushed off the little rocks, forcing myself to continue, hoping I was going in the right direction. After six or seven blocks, panic rose in my chest. I scanned the buildings and couldn't see any that were familiar. I closed my eyes and said a silent prayer. When I opened them, recognition dawned. I knew the fence to my left. I'd stared at it day after day, albeit from a different angle. It was the same fence I had watched Mary climb when she'd visited. Beyond the fence, I could make out the roofline of my house. Both relief and fear enveloped me.

Although the doctor had said he would delay Richard as long as he could, I didn't know if he'd been successful. Plus, I'd been wandering the streets for a long time, maybe as much as an hour. In that time, Richard could have left the hospital and come home. Another thought hit me. The man he had watching the house could still be there.

Tears sprung to my eyes. I felt overwhelmed, like I couldn't do it. It was too much. But I looked down and saw the roundness of my belly and shook my head. I couldn't let him have my child. He or she would know their mother. I took a deep breath and prepared myself. I was going to have to run for it. I couldn't accomplish what I had planned without going into that house first.

Nodding, I stepped out and crossed the street. I snuck along the fence to the front of the house, looked in the windows, and saw blackness. I scanned the street opposite me, squinting against the darkness to examine the area below the pecan tree. Nobody stood there. I looked to where Charles kept his horse, but saw nothing. I sprang to the front door, opened it, and quickly closed it behind me. I stood, listening. Waiting. At any point, I expected him to grab me. But nothing. Keeping the house dark, I moved down the hallway, my hand running along the wall to guide me. I reached our bedroom and opened the closet door. I grabbed my overnight bag, the one I had packed for this very thing, and shut the door, sure to leave everything as I had found it.

Now for the last step. I went to the kitchen, found a candle and matches, and opened the door to the cellar. I stepped on the top step, closed the door, and lit a match. The light burst from the tip, and I lit the candle. It was a faint glow, but it gave me what I needed. It was six steps to the bottom, and I counted them as I descended.

When I was down here, weeks ago, I had noticed a safe in the corner. Curious, I searched for the key. Under a jar of peaches on the shelf, I found it. The key fit the lock. Inside was a lot of cash. Worrying Richard might come home and see me, I never counted it. But I knew it was more than enough to get me to my destination, provided it was still there.

I set down my overnight bag, went to the shelf, and lifted the peach jar. I exhaled with relief. It was still there. Now I could only hope the cash was still in the safe. I went to it, turned the key, and looked inside. My greatest hopes were fulfilled. The safe was even more full than the last time I had checked. I set down the candle, grabbed my bag, and stuffed it with cash. So much cash I could barely fit it all in the bag.

When I was finished, I closed the safe door, replaced the key, and climbed the stairs when I heard a noise. It was the front door to the house. Richard had returned.

I blew out the candle and didn't trust myself to move. I stood still on the steps in the cellar, listening. The front door shut, and I could hear his footsteps. The wood floor creaked under his weight. His movement grew louder, and I thought he was heading to the kitchen, but he stopped. When the steps started again, they were moving away from me. I could barely hear him. He was on the other side of the house. Occasionally, I heard a random sound, but nothing consistent. He was too far away for me to know what he was doing.

A thought came to me. What if I ran for it? He was as far from the front door as he could get. I almost opened the door and flew as fast as my pregnant body would carry me, but wisdom took over. I knew I'd never make it. Even if I got out of the house, he'd be on me in seconds. There was no way I'd be able to outrun him. If he was home for the night, I'd have to wait until he went to sleep to sneak out.

His footsteps grew louder again, and I knew he was coming down the hall. I prayed he would retrace his steps to the front door and exit, but he didn't. He entered the kitchen. He was only feet away from me. Light streamed through the gap under the door, and I could hear him moving around. I looked at the candle in my hand and wondered. Would he notice? Would he see it was missing? My heart beat so fast I worried he could hear it. I was barely breathing, holding my breath as much as possible. Admonishing myself to stay calm. He stepped to the cellar door, and I saw his shadow in the light gap. He knew. I considered what I could do when he opened the door. How I could free myself. But the door didn't open. Instead, the light went out, and his footsteps moved off. I could hear him in the front room. The creak of the front door opening lifted my spirits. Moments later, he shut it, and the house was silent.

I exhaled, taking deep breaths. Quietly, I climbed the last step and slowly opened the door. The house was dark. I placed the candle back on the counter, went to the front window, and carefully looked out. He was on his horse, riding away. Tears of joy sprang to my eyes. For the first time, I thought I might actually get away from him.

I waited several seconds, making sure he was gone, then opened the front door, carrying my bag. I crept along the shadows, staying off the road, and getting distance from him and the house. I walked several blocks back toward downtown. I wasn't sure where I'd go, but I needed to stay out of sight for several hours. At six a.m., provided Mary had completed her last task, my ride would be waiting for me at the Thorn Hotel. The last time we met, in my kitchen, she assured me she would arrange a ride for me. Now, she's missing and I can only hope she fulfilled her promise before Richard got her.

Chapter 38

Louise

I can't remember ever being more tired. Once, when I was little, Mother had let me and Barbara walk to my friend Anna's house. She lived two miles away, and it was July. By the time we arrived, we were tired and sweaty. We knocked on the door, but nobody answered. Anna was supposed to be home. We had planned it, but she had to leave and had no way to tell us. We sat waiting under the maple tree in front of her house, but after thirty minutes, Barbara convinced me to turn back for home. We made the two-mile walk back in hundred-degree heat with no water. Four miles round trip with no water in July, for two girls younger than eight.

When we finally reached home, I threw off my shoes and dunked my head in water. I lay under the elm tree behind our house and never thought I'd move again. My little legs were completely exhausted.

That was nothing compared to how I felt that night in Austin. I hadn't slept in twenty-four hours. I was as big as a house, with child, and my husband was out there somewhere, hunting for me with bad intentions. What was perhaps the most difficult in the whole thing was that there was a hotel right across the street from me with rooms to rent. It rose from the ground like a wicked temptation, beckoning me to enter. I never gave in, not because I couldn't afford it. But because I couldn't run the risk. Visions of Richard standing over me in a Colorado Springs hotel room ran through my mind, warning me. Richard was a well-connected man. He could have spies everywhere. Plus, even if they didn't mean to, people would remember the big pregnant woman who checked into the hotel alone. No, I had to stay out there. Agonizingly close. The last time anyone saw me was leaving the hospital. Nobody, including the doctor, knew where I had been since. That knowledge was comforting.

I looked down at my watch. It was hard to make out the hands in the dark, although every minute more light filled the sky above. At five minutes to six in the morning, my anxiety and fatigue seemed to reach an all-time high. My ride was supposed to arrive at six. When last Mary and I spoke, she was going to ride out of town to Taylor Station and arrange a ride for me. She said she had a cousin out there and would have him meet me outside the Thorn Hotel. He'd give me a ride out of town to the train station. I'd be on a train headed out of Austin before Richard had even realized I was gone.

Our original plan had me sneaking out in the middle of the night. Mary would meet me and bring me here. But yesterday, she never showed up, and Richard said I'd never see her again. I didn't know what he did to her, but at that point, I could only hope she made it to her cousin.

The clip-clop of the horse's hooves brought me from my thoughts. I looked across the street and saw a covered wagon pulling up in front of the hotel. A man sat on the seat holding the reins. I looked around, stepped out from the shadows, and walked toward the wagon. The man saw my movement and turned to look at me. We immediately recognized each other. He was the same man who had brought me to town when I had first arrived at Taylor Station.

"You're Mary's cousin?" I asked.

He nodded and jumped down to the street, looking around. "Where's Mary?"

I shook my head. "I'm not sure."

He stared at me, clenching and unclenching his jaw. I worried he might send me away, but he didn't. He took my bag, then extended his other hand and helped me up on the wagon. "Sit in the back, out of sight."

That was already my plan, and I crawled over the seat and into the back. He swung my bag back to me, and I touched it, feeling relieved to have it by my side.

"Didn't I tell you to go home to Chicago?" He asked.

Not waiting for a reply, he sat in the wagon seat, snapped the reins, and we began to slowly move down Fifth Street.

After several blocks, he leaned his head inside the canvas and asked over the rattle of the wagon, "When did you last see Mary?"

"Two days ago."

He bit his lip and shut the canvas again. Ten minutes went by without either of us speaking. The initial excitement of his arrival wore off, and my eyes grew heavy. I leaned against the frame of the wagon and fell asleep. I didn't know how long I was out, but a sharp pain in my ribs woke me. A cramp seized my stomach, and my entire front felt like electric pulses were running through the muscles. I forced myself to breathe, taking short, quick breaths. After several seconds, it finally passed.

"Gerald?"

He said nothing.

I called out louder. "Gerald?"

"Huh?" he said, leaning his head through the wagon cover.

"Do you have water?"

He reached down, handed me a canteen, and turned back. I took several large gulps and leaned back. The wagon slowed, then stopped. He leaned his head through the canvas again.

"Stay hidden, but I think your husband might be waiting for us at the station. What does he look like?"

"Wavy, dark hair, blue eyes, muscular build."

"Riding a brown mare with white spots?"

"Yes."

"Yep, that's him. Stay down. There's a blanket back there. Lay on the floor and put it over you."

He snapped the reins, and my body screamed in protest as I rolled off the seat and sat on the ground, bracing myself. Forgetting the largeness of my belly, I struggled to reach for the blanket but finally gripped it and lay back, pulling it over my body. As if the wagon weren't already hot enough, I lay on the floor with a blanket over me. I felt as if I might burst into a ball of fire. Sweating profusely, I considered pulling off the blanket when I heard Gerald call out a greeting. The wagon slowed, then stopped, and I heard Richard's voice. Through the cracks in the wagon, I could see the legs of Richard's mare.

"Howdy, sir. You from around here?"

"Yup."

"I'm looking for a woman. Dark hair, young, very pregnant."

"Out here on the road?"

"Maybe. She was in Austin. She has some mental problems, and I'm trying to find her."

"Hmm, and she came this way?"

"I think so."

"Well, I ain't seen any woman like that. I'll keep my eyes out for her, though."

Suddenly, pain worse than before erupted from my belly. I reached my right hand up and covered my mouth, but not before a gasp escaped my lips.

"What was that?" Richard asked.

I closed my eyes, focusing on my breathing, keeping as silent as possible, fighting the pain, and hoping he didn't hear.

"This wagon creaks," Gerald said and snapped the reins. We began moving, but Richard stayed beside the wagon.

"Where are you coming from?"

"San Antonio."

"Where are you headed?"

"Home. I think the horses can smell the barn. We're close now, and it's been a tough journey. Best of luck finding the woman."

We continued down the road, me under the blanket fighting labor pains when Gerald pushed his head through the canvas.

"What happened?"

"I'm sorry," I said through gritted teeth. "I think I'm going into labor." Another pain struck, and I gasped, gritting my teeth. "Are we close to your house?"

"Yup, just up the road. But your husband's following us."

Chapter 39

Louise

We turned off the road and traveled down the long path leading to the house. I was on my knees; the labor pains were coming five minutes apart. Every bump of the wagon made it worse.

"Almost there," he said, seeing I was barely hanging on.

"What about my husband?"

Gerald looked back.

"Looks like he's out on the road. We'll be out of sight in a couple of minutes. That should give us enough time to get you into the house."

I heard a couple of dogs barking and knew we were only paces away. Gerald swung the wagon as close to the front of the house as possible.

"I'm sorry, but you're going to have to climb over the seat. The wagon will block the door to the house. Stay on the house side of the wagon, just in case he's watching."

Another wave of pain struck, clenching every one of my stomach muscles. After several seconds that felt like more, I relaxed and gritted my teeth, climbing over the seat. Gerald sat on the outside blocking me, and a woman stood on the other side on the ground. She was middle-aged with long, curly, brown hair that was going gray. Her eyes were kind, concerned.

"Come on, dear. Let me help you."

She reached up and gripped my hand, helping me down.

"My bag," I said.

She put an arm around me and looked back up at her husband. "Gerald, her bag."

He reached into the wagon, grabbed my bag, and handed it to her. I knew another wave of pain would come soon, and I needed to get in the house. She carried my bag and supported me with the other arm. I waddled to the front door, climbing the steps. I opened the door and entered their front room. A couch was on one side, and she helped me to it.

"How far apart are they?" she asked.

"Four minutes."

Gerald came in after us and shut the door. Another wave of contractions struck, and I gripped the couch cushions. I was barely aware of them standing over me, watching. But I could hear them whispering to each other.

"A train will come into the station in just a few minutes," Gerald said. "I have to be there."

"I know," his wife said. "We'll do our best."

I watched as he took a pistol from his holster and handed it to her.

"If that man comes in, shoot him. Don't hesitate."

Gerald opened the door and was gone as my stomach relaxed. His wife kneeled in front of me, her face pressed to mine.

"Barbara, I'm Anne Marie. Do you think you could walk just a little more?"

Tears streamed down my face, but I nodded, and she helped me up. I leaned on her as we walked down the hall and entered a bedroom. She helped me onto the bed, and I lay back. My tears and sweat-filled hair covered the pillows. She held my hand, looking down at me.

"I'm going to get some water and towels. I'll be right back."

She moved to walk away, but I kept hold of her hand. "Have you ever delivered a baby?"

She shook her head and smiled. "But I have five of my own. All were born right here, in this house. I might be just as scared as you are, but we're going to get through this together."

Chapter 40

Louise

I sat on the train, looking out the window. It had been an hour since I'd boarded, and I could feel the brakes engage, indicating we were reaching our first stop, Taylor Station. I looked down at the bundle in my arms. My son, Jacob, was sleeping soundly, wrapped in pink blankets and wearing a bow on top of his head. The pink blankets and bow were Anne Marie's idea. She suggested them right before I left.

"I was thinking," she said as we sat at the kitchen table in her house, "you should dress Jacob like a girl."

I looked at her strangely. "What? Why?"

"Think about it. It's another way to throw Richard off the trail. When you reach your destination, you'll eventually need to dress him in boy's clothes and blankets. But as you travel, he could be a girl. Richard doesn't know you've had a boy. If he asks anyone who might see you on the train, they'd say a woman was traveling with a baby girl. In your new home, Jacob will be a boy. If he ever somehow tracks you, he'll be looking for you and a little girl."

She smiled and pulled a pink blanket from behind her back.

After helping me dress him, we walked out of the house through the front door. It was the first time in a week the sun had touched my face, and it was glorious. I never knew how much I missed the sun and the freedom it provided. The last couple of months of being a prisoner in my house gave me a new appreciation. When we exited, the wagon was pulled up close to the front door, blocking the view from the road. Although Richard hadn't been seen since the day we had arrived, Gerald wasn't taking any chances.

Holding Jacob in my arms, I turned and hugged Anne Marie. "Thank you," I whispered. It felt incredibly inadequate for what she had done for me. I owed her my life and my son's. Without her, I didn't know what would have happened to us. Words couldn't express the gratitude I felt. When I released her, I noticed tears in her eyes.

"I'll write when I arrive," I promised.

She nodded. "From Kansas City. But not from Denver. Never from Denver."

I agreed, climbed into the wagon, lay in the back with Jacob, and felt the wagon move. We traveled south through Austin, while I fought the temptation to look out the wagon's cover at the town I had called home but would never see again.

Two nights before, the three of us had discussed where I might go. We knew I had to leave and get as much distance as possible. Anne Marie suggested I go back to my family in Chicago, but I dismissed it. That would be the first place Richard would check.

"What about Denver?" Gerald asked.

"Denver?" I said.

"Yes."

"Why?"

He raised his knee up and crossed one foot over the other. "Where is the one place Richard would never go?"

"Denver," Anne Marie said.

He turned and looked at her. "Exactly. He's wanted for murder there. He has to be frightened at the thought of going back. It's also somewhere he would never expect you to go. You've never been there. You need to go somewhere he wouldn't look. Why not Denver?"

That night, we also agreed I shouldn't leave from Taylor Station. Richard hadn't been seen again since the first day, but another man had. I suspected he was the same man who had watched my house from below the pecan tree. The closest train station was south of Austin, which meant we'd need to travel through before I could head north.

Once we were past the city limits, I left Jacob sleeping in the back of the wagon and climbed onto the seat next to Gerald.

"Nice to be out of the house?" he asked.

"Nice...and scary."

He moved his eyes back to the road. "How are you feeling?"

"Physically? Good."

"You'll see a doctor when you reach Denver, right? Make sure everything's okay?"

"I will."

I looked away, out over the rolling hills.

"Speaking of doctors, can I ask you to do one more thing for me?"

"Of course," he said, turning his head.

"Will you thank Dr. Frieberg for me? Without him, I never would have gotten away."

He turned back, and our eyes locked.

"Yup. Gladly."

I hesitated before the next question, but I had to know. "What about Mary?"

He frowned and looked down, snapping the reins. "Nothing."

Tears brimmed my eyelids. He looked back up at me.

"Barbara, it's not your fault. It's Richard's. She wanted to help you, and she did. Someday he'll pay for whatever he did to her. The best thing you can do is get away and raise that baby back there to be nothing like his father."

The train stopped, and I looked back out the window. I should have sat on the other side of the train, kept my head down, and waited until we had pulled away, but I didn't. Only two people, both women, stood on the platform. The one climbed aboard, while the other stood back by the building. She looked at me, and our eyes locked. I couldn't believe it. How was it possible? The relief I felt overwhelmed me and tears sprang to my eyes. She was letting me know she was okay. The train whistle sounded, and it began pulling away. Neither of us moved. Our eyes locked on each other until she finally stepped out of sight.

Chapter 41

Michael

Michael sits on the couch in the comfortable home of Dr. Frieberg and waits. Frieberg's wife, Marie, said the doctor would be home soon and readily agreed to let Michael inside. That was thirty minutes ago. Since, they'd been sitting in the front room, chit-chatting, with Michael wishing he had waited outside. The conversation comprised her talking and him listening. Michael found she was the type of person to ask a question only because she wanted to see it returned. When he would reciprocate, she would go on long dissertations about subjects he knew little about. Many included names of family or friends Michael would have no way of knowing. Twice he had subtly checked his watch, winning frowns from Marie.

He hears footsteps on the porch and thinks an angelic choir couldn't sound more glorious.

Dr. Frieberg enters and moves down the hall to the back of the house.

"Honey? In here," Marie calls out.

Frieberg enters the kitchen.

Marie turns to Michael and smiles.

"Sorry, one minute."

She stands and leaves the room, going after him. Michael hears their muffled voices.

"Theodore, we have company."

"What?"

Marie drops her voice, and Michael can't hear the words.

"Who?" Dr. Frieberg asks.

Again, Marie's muffled response.

Now both voices are low and indistinguishable. After a few seconds, Frieberg, with Marie trailing, enters the room.

"Theodore Frieberg," he says, extending his hand.

Michael stands. "Michael Delaney."

"Please, sit back down."

Frieberg and his wife sit opposite Michael on the loveseat. It's an awkward image because Frieberg is a large man with long legs that seem to go on and on. Sitting on the low loveseat makes his knees reach his chest. Michael has the large couch to himself.

"My wife tells me you're from Denver."

"I am."

"And you're a detective?"

"That's right."

Frieberg looks at Marie, who nods.

"Well, I must say, your visit has me curious. I've never been to Denver. I'd like to see the mountains. I hear they're beautiful."

"They are." Michael looks at his watch. "I don't want to take up too much of your time. I've already done that to Marie." She waves her hand and opens her mouth to respond, but Michael doesn't have the patience to get her started again. "I'm here because I have some questions about a former patient of yours."

"Oh?"

"Barbara Amhurst."

Frieberg freezes. His friendly tone goes hard when he speaks.

"Mr. Delaney, do you have a badge? Something that validates who you are?"

Michael nods and pulls it from his pocket. He holds it out for Frieberg, who examines it and leans back in satisfaction. When he speaks, his tone is no longer firm but morose.

"Did he find her?"

"Who?"

"Richard."

Michael shakes his head. "No, not to my knowledge."

Frieberg exhales. "Well, that's a relief. So, why are you here?"

"I'm looking for her."

"Huh? You haven't found her?"

"No."

"Hmm. Why are you looking for her?"

Michael tells him about the murdered woman in Denver. About looking for a man who met Richard's description. About finding Richard in the Kansas City jailhouse. About the mayor in Kansas City, his first trip to Austin, and his most recent trip to Chicago.

"I've heard you were one of the last people to see her here. I was hoping you could tell me what happened."

The doctor leans forward and grimaces. "One of the strangest situations I've ever seen. Her husband visited me one day. He said his wife was pregnant, and he'd like me to be her doctor. He told me they were keeping her pregnancy quiet and asked if I wouldn't mind doing my visits at the house. He offered double my normal rate. I thought it strange but agreed. At first, everything was normal. I'd go over, check on Babara, and leave. Things were progressing nicely in the pregnancy."

He leans back and crosses his legs.

"One day, I go to the house and nobody answers. I returned the next day, and still nobody was home. I looked inside the windows but saw nothing amiss and assumed they'd left town suddenly. A week later, Amhurst returned to my office and told me Barbara had to leave suddenly to visit her family out of town. She was back now, and he wanted me to check on her. I agreed and said I'd come the next day. When I did, Amhurst was there. It was odd because he had never been before. I continued coming each week, and each time he was there. It was as if she couldn't talk without getting permission from him first. He was watching her."

Frieberg shakes his head. "That first time, when he was there, there were abrasions on her wrists and ankles. Like she'd been tied up."

Marie takes a sharp breath.

"Why didn't you do something?" Michael asks.

Frieberg looks at his wife, then back at Michael. "It's not the first time I've seen something like that." He looks back at her. "Some couples have...different activities than others." He turns back to Michael. "Anyway, I continued to visit her, but saw no further indications of abuse. Something felt wrong, though. I just didn't have any proof to support my fears. Finally, one night, Amhurst called me in a panic and said his wife was ill and bleeding everywhere. I rushed over and found her in bed. Blood was all over the bathroom floor."

He shakes his head.

"I could see it was staged. Her actions seemed forced. To me, a doctor who had delivered many babies in trying circumstances, I didn't buy it. Plus, there wasn't any fresh blood. It was like someone had dumped blood on the floor and spread it on her legs. But, knowing what I knew, I went with it. I rushed her to the hospital. I made her husband stay in the front, and I questioned her. That's when she told me he was going to kill her. He was only keeping her alive to get the baby. She was petrified. That was her only chance at escape."

"And you believed her?"

"Yes."

"Then what happened?"

"She snuck out the back, and I went to the front. I told Amhurst that his wife was very ill and her life was in danger. I'd do all I could, but she and the baby might not make it. That's when he became irate. He threatened me, telling me if I didn't save the baby, he'd hold me responsible. I had to have a few men restrain him. They took him outside to prevent him from going back to see her. When I returned, she was gone."

"When did he realize he had been duped?"

"In the morning. He demanded to see her. That's when I told him that some-time in the night, she snuck away."

"What did he do?"

"He came unglued. He struck me, then left. I saw him ride away on his horse. All I could do was pray he didn't find her. From the sounds of it, he never did."

"Where did Barbara go?"

"A man from out of town picked her up in a wagon. He took her to his house, where she had the baby."

"Did Richard know?"

"Not that I know of. If he did, she wouldn't have made it away."

Michael makes a couple of notes in his notepad, then turns back to the doctor.

"Any idea where Barbara went after the baby?"

The doctor laughs. "You'll never believe it."

"Why?"

"Because, if you're really looking for her, you'd have a better chance of finding her in your hometown than here."

"What, why?"

"Because that's where she went. She headed to Denver."

Michael frowns. "What?"

"That's right. At least, that's what I was told. She's teaching school there." He smiled. "Maybe she's teaching your kids."

Michael stares at him. "One last question."

"What?"

"What was Richard's motive? What did he want from her?"

"The baby."

"Why?"

Frieberg purses his lips. "I asked myself the same question. For days, I pondered over it. When he thought Barbara was in trouble, his only concern was for the baby. Nothing else mattered. He didn't care if she died. He wanted the baby for control. Everything in Richard's life was about control. Everything was for his gratification and needs. If they didn't fulfill them, they weren't valuable. Richard wanted something he could raise and manipulate. Someone with his genetics. I can only imagine what he had planned for that little boy."

They stare at each other for several seconds, then Michael stands and extends his hand. The doctor takes it.

"Thank you for your help."

"You're welcome." He grips Michael's shoulder as Michael turns toward the door. "Promise me, if you find her, please keep her safe."

"I will."

"Are you headed there now?"

"I have one more stop here. I need to talk to Mr. Fredricks again. The hotel owner."

"Oh..."

"What?"

"I'm sorry to tell you. He died of a heart attack last night."

Chapter 42

Louise

"Mrs. McKenna?"

I turn away from the blackboard and look at the student with his hand raised.

"Yes, Billy. What is it?"

"Must we do the spelling bee?"

I finish writing the sentence before answering. When I'm done, I turn back and look at the children. Every little face looks back at me, and I can tell by their anxious looks, he's speaking for all of them. I put the chalk on the tray and move forward.

"Have I ever told you about the first class I taught?"

Several heads shake.

"It was here, in this school. I just moved in and needed a job. I heard that the school might be looking for a teacher, and I spoke with the principal. He invited me back the next day. He said one teacher was very sick and might not return for months. When I left his office, I was excited. Not because the teacher was sick, but because I needed a job. But once I had time to think about it, I got nervous. Have any of you ever felt nervous before?"

Several heads bob up and down. I can see I have their full attention.

"Well, that night, I thought about what I might teach. I came up with this plan and felt much better. I came here to the school early the next morning, and when I walked into the classroom, the principal was there. He welcomed me and told me he had a lesson he wanted me to teach. It wasn't what I had prepared. Guess what he wanted me to talk about?"

"What?" all the kids ask in unison.

"Who knows what photosynthesis is?"

Maybell in the front raises her hand. "Is it something with plants?"

"Yes, exactly. All I knew was that it had something to do with how a plant grows."

I walk to the other side of the room, their little heads following me.

"So, then, the kids, like all of you, started coming into the class. I thought the principal might leave, but he didn't. He stayed to watch me. I was so nervous. I wanted to run right out of the room."

"What did you do?" Henry asks from the back of the class.

"I stood up in front of the class, introduced myself, and asked them the same question I just asked you. What is photosynthesis? And guess what?"

"What?" they ask in unison.

"One boy in the class, Jonathan, loved science and loved to talk about it. He raised his hand and told the class what it was. That gave me an idea. I could just ask questions, and Jonathan could answer them if I got stuck. And you know what? It worked. Nobody in the class knew, including the principal, that I knew nothing about photosynthesis. So why do you think I tell you all this story?"

They look at me, then look around at each other.

"Because I know you're nervous about the spelling bee. And I know you don't want to get something wrong and think maybe people will laugh if you do. But guess what? There are plenty of words I still spell wrong, and I'm the teacher. Do you know I'm actually glad the principal asked me to teach on photosynthesis?"

"You are?" Sarah says.

"Yes. Because after that, I got a book and read all about it. I studied everything I could to know all about photosynthesis. And guess what? If you get out in the spelling bee, I promise you, whatever word you miss, you'll remember forever. It's a great way to learn an unfamiliar word."

I smile at them, and they smile back. I know I've reached them.

A couple of hours later, once school is over, I sit at my desk, preparing for the next day of lessons, when Principal Todd enters the room. I look up from the desk and start to stand, but he stops me with a wave of his hand. He walks over and leans on one of the small desks.

"How was class today?"

I put down my pencil and look at him.

"Fantastic. Really fun. The kids were nervous about the spelling bee, and I seemed to ease their concerns. I felt like I reached them. It was a significant moment."

"You know we love you here, Beverly. Your coming has been a great addition to the school."

"Thank you for giving me the chance. I love it here."

He looks away and rubs his chin, and my heart drops.

"You know, I've never really asked you where you came from or how you got here. I didn't feel like it mattered."

I can feel my cheeks heat up, and I nod.

"A man came here today. He asked me some questions about you."

I can feel my heart beating hard.

"I wouldn't tell him much, and he left. He wanted to come see you, but I told him you were busy with a class. He seemed adamant, but eventually, he left."

"I..."

He holds up a hand. "I don't need an explanation. I know who you are. You've been wonderful for the school, and your class loves you. I don't know where you came from or why. As far as I'm concerned, it has no bearing on your position here. I just wanted you to know about the man."

"Thank you, Mr. Todd."

He nods and moves toward the door.

"What did he look like?"

"Maybe mid-thirties, sandy-brown hair, thick beard."

"What color were his eyes?"

"Blue."

Fear grips me. "Thank you."

He walks out, and I jump up from the desk, stuff my bag with my things, and rush out. I've got to get home. I've got to check on Jacob.

Chapter 43

Louise

I stand in the ticket line, tapping my foot and looking over my shoulder. I check the large board of arrivals and departures and wonder what destination I should choose. The woman in front of me turns around and smiles, then looks down at Jacob standing beside me, holding my hand.

"He's so cute."

"Thank you."

"I've never seen eyes like that." She examines my eyes and looks at my left hand holding my bag, before looking back down at him. "Are your husband's eyes blue like that?"

I don't know how many times I've been asked a question like this, and I give the same answer I always have.

"No, he's the only one."

"So unique."

The attendant calls out, "Next in line," and the woman turns around and walks up to the counter. Jacob looks up at me, and I smile down at him. The woman finishes, and I struggle to the counter with Jacob holding my right hand and a large bag in the other. The woman behind the counter smiles at me. I've got my hands full, and she can see it.

"How can I help you?"

"I'd like a ticket to Los Angeles, please."

"Oh, I'm sorry, dear. We just sold out." My face falls, and she reaches out and touches my hand. "But we have another train this afternoon."

I turn and look over my shoulder at the line behind me and the other people in the station. *Would I recognize the man who's looking for us if I saw him?* I scan the faces, seeing several men with beards, but most are older than mid-thirties.

"Dear? Do you want that ticket for four p.m. to Los Angeles?"

I turn back and look at her. "What's the next available train?"

She looks down at her list of departures.

"Oh, I'm sorry. It's headed in the other direction to Kansas City."

I turn and check over my shoulder one more time before nodding.

"Two tickets to Kansas City, please."

She frowns. "Are you sure?"

"I am."

She smiles. "I'll only charge you for one." She motions to Jacob. "I bet he's going to be on your lap most of the time, anyway."

I smile and thank her, taking the tickets and walking to the platform. The train is parked on the track, ready to leave, and we walk to the appropriate door and climb the stairs. Jacob scrambles up the steps in front of me as I squeeze our large bag through the stairwell. An attendant greets us, takes our tickets, and offers to carry my bag as we move to our seats.

He walks us past several rows of people reading newspapers, books, or conversing. With Jacob holding my hand, we follow him. He walks to the front of the car and points to the two seats in the first row. Four seats are on either side of the aisle, and a pair of grandparents are seated on the window side of us. The attendant puts our bag in the rack above the seat, and I encourage Jacob to sit in the middle next to the grandmotherly woman. He shakes his head, reaching up to me, and I sit down in the aisle seat and pick him up, holding him on my lap.

The attendant leaves us, and I look at the smiling older woman as Jacob buries his head into my shoulder.

"First time on a train?" she asks.

"For me?"

She nods.

"No."

▢"What about for him?"

"Yes. Well, actually, no, not for him either. He traveled on one when he was a baby. But he wouldn't remember."

Jacob, sensing we're talking about him, looks up at me, then at her.

"Well, hello, young man. What's your name?"

He stares at her, then buries his head into my chest.

"Jacob," I tell her.

"He has such big, beautiful eyes." She checks mine, then looks at him again. "Nice to meet you, Jacob."

He turns away from her and squeezes me tighter.

"He's shy," I explain.

She smiles. "I'm Cheryl."

Before I can answer, she looks up at something behind me. I turn to see what she's looking at and stare right into the face of a man with blue eyes and a thick, sandy-brown beard.

"Hello, Louise," he says. "Do you mind if I join you for just a minute?"

He doesn't wait for a response and sits down in Jacob's seat, between me and the old woman. As he does, I feel the shift in the train and know we're moving. He nods to the woman beside him and turns back to me. I consider jumping up and making a run for it.

"My name is Michael Delaney," he says. He reaches into his pocket, pulls out a police badge, and shows it to me. "I've been looking for you for a long time. I'm so glad to have found you."

Jacob, feeling my anxiety, raises his head from my chest and looks at me with curiosity.

"I'm sorry to surprise you like this, but I didn't know how else to reach you. I waited outside the school, but you never came out. I thought you might end up here. I guess I was right." He chuckles.

What am I supposed to say? What am I supposed to think?

"I've been tracking the man you know as Charles, or Richard, for several years. I first learned about you on a visit to Austin."

The train is moving fast along the tracks now, and I feel my head has been detached from my body. I look past him and see the older couple watching the interchange with curiosity. The man asks me, "Miss, do you know this man?"

I shake my head, and Michael turns to them, showing his badge.

"I've been looking for these two for quite a while. She's not in trouble or anything. I'm here to help them. She's a very brave woman."

I don't know what it is about the comment, but it breaks some imaginary floodgates I've built inside. A barricade I've constructed against my emotions.

The couple looks from him, then back to me as my eyes well up with tears. A sob erupts from me, and Jacob leans back, looks up at me, then cries himself. I try to control my sobs, but the more I fight for control, the harder they come. I'm aware of others looking at me now. The train attendant who had helped us get seated comes over, and Michael shows his badge.

"Can we go somewhere more private to talk?" Michael asks him.

The attendant has us follow him. I stand, holding Jacob in my arms, and motion for my bag. Michael takes it down and offers to carry it for me.

"Mama?" Jacob asks as we start down the aisle behind the attendant.

"It's okay," I tell him, smiling against the tears.

I wipe my eyes and follow the attendant as people stare at us. We enter another car with a different configuration of seats, and I recognize it as a dining car. The attendant motions to a secluded spot away from other guests, and I sit down, struggling to squeeze between the seat and the table with Jacob clinging to me. Micheal sits on the other side, and the attendant leaves.

"Jacob, honey, can you sit down next to Mama?"

I slide him off of me to the seat next to the window. Michael holds out a white handkerchief, and I take it, blowing my nose and wiping my eyes.

"Sorry," I say.

"What could you possibly be sorry for?"

We stare at each other, then I offer the handkerchief back, but he tells me to keep it.

I take a big breath and look up at him. "So, who are you?"

"My name is Michael Delaney. I'm a detective with the Denver police. I've been looking for your husband since he murdered his first wife here. I found him in Kansas City and have been investigating his life since he left here."

The mention of Kansas City strikes fear in my heart, and Michael sees it.

"Don't worry. He's in jail in Kansas City. He can't hurt you."

I nod and take a deep breath.

"For the longest time, I thought you were dead," Micheal says, smiling. "I can't believe I've found you. You didn't make it easy."

"I guess I didn't do enough."

A server comes over and asks us if we want anything to eat.

"Are you hungry?" Michael asks me.

I shake my head, and he waves away the server. But before he leaves, I call him back. I ask him for milk for Jacob, and he walks away.

Michael looks at Jacob, then at me. "He has his eyes."

I nod.

"I met your mother in Chicago."

"You did?"

He nods. "She believed you were still alive. She was right."

We stare at each other.

"Did you put him in jail?"

He shakes his head. "It's not murder that landed him there."

"No?"

He looks at my bag. "It's that."

"What?" I say, reaching over and gripping the bag.

"The money," he says, dropping his voice. "Don't worry. I'm not going to take it. As far as I'm concerned, you earned it. Plus, the man who really has a claim to it is dead."

"Who's that?"

"The man who took over the hotel after Charles...left." He says the last word with contempt.

"He left Austin?"

Michael nods. "Near as I can tell, he left right after you. I think he knew you went to Kansas City but then lost you." He smiles, chuckling. "Pretty clever going to Denver. I didn't figure out that part. It was the doctor who told me."

"Dr. Frieberg?"

Michael nods.

I sit back in the seat and shake my head. He knows everything.

"So why find me?"

The smile leaves his face, and he leans forward. "I need you."

"For what?"

"You remember how I said the hotel owner is dead?"

"Yes. Did Charles kill him?"

"Well, you could argue he did. But not in the classical sense. Anyway, he just recently died, and once they find out in Kansas City, they may not be able to keep him."

"You mean he'll be let out?"

Michael nods.

"But how? He's killed all these women. His first wife, Mary, the girl he was dating before me, his aunt and uncle..."

"There isn't any evidence, though. Nothing that proves he killed them. But you, you're different. You got away. You survived. I want you to come to Kansas City with me. Talk to the mayor and the sheriff. Tell them your story."

I don't even have to think about my response. "No."

"No?"

"I got away from him. I'll disappear. He won't find me."

He crosses his arms and stares at me. "For how long?"

"What?"

"How long, Louise? How long until he finds you? Maybe he never will. But are you sure? I did. You and I both know he won't rest until he finds you and Jacob. For the rest of your life, you'll be out there somewhere, looking over your shoulder, wondering if that man walking down the street is him."

I stare at him and know he's right. But the thought of going back, telling someone who I am and what he did to me is too much.

The server comes back and gives me a cup of milk, and I slide it over to Jacob. He grabs for it, and I help him as he gulps down several swallows. When he's done, I hand him a toy car, and he begins rolling it around the table. I look back at Michael.

"I'm sorry," I say, shaking my head. "I can't."

He nods. I see the look of disappointment on his face. He leans back and puts his arms up on the seat. After a few seconds, he says, "Will you do one thing for me then?"

I look at him warily. "What?"

"Go see your mother. Tell her you're alive."

Chapter 44

Michael

Michael walks into the Kansas City courthouse, makes eye contact with the man seated at the table reading the newspaper, then turns and goes down the stairs. When he reaches the basement, he notices the jailer sitting on a chair outside the row of iron bars. Like the last time he was here, the man is asleep.

"Morning, Ron."

Ron startles awake and looks up, fighting to focus his eyes.

"I'm back to visit Johns again."

Ron rubs his cheek. "Okay."

"Can I see him in the same room as before?"

Ron nods, standing slowly from the chair. He pulls the large ring of keys from his belt and inserts the right one in the lock, turning it with ease. "Do you remember where it is?"

Michael tells him he does and moves to the room. He opens the door and closes it behind himself as Ron relocks the gate, then retreats down the hall. Michael sits in the chair he had occupied last time. A minute later, Johns enters the room, his hands shackled in front of him. Ron follows him in. Michael and Johns make eye contact, a slight smirk on Johns's face. Ron points to the chair and Johns sits down.

"Want me to stay?" Ron asks Michael.

"No, we should be okay."

Ron looks again at Johns, then closes the door, pulling it shut behind him.

The two men look at each other, but this time, Johns speaks with no prompting.

"How was my hotel?"

Michael leans back as the electric blue eyes dance.

"Looked good. You'd be pleased."

"Is Johnny still working the front desk?"

Michael nods. He never knew the name of the man who had welcomed him to the hotel, but assumes he must be Johnny, considering he knew the man who sits across from Michael now. They watch each other, and Michael can't help his surprise. It's as if he's seeing a totally new person. The last two times he had come, Johns never opened his mouth. Now, he's treating him like an old friend. *Why the change?*

Johns leans forward and drops his voice. "So, what do you want to know? Why I did it?"

"Did what?" Michael asks.

"Killed Helen."

Michael stares back at him. Helen was Johns's first wife. Michael nods.

Johns leans back and puts his shackled hands on the table. "We were married for a year. An entire year I wasted on that girl. I humped her," he looks up at the ceiling, "I can't even count how many times, and that worthless trash never got pregnant. Then she had the audacity to blame me. Well, that was it. I have no patience for anyone who can't accept responsibility."

"So, you killed her?"

Johns nods. "It was time to leave Denver anyway, and she was holding me back. She became so needy and emotional. I couldn't stand to be near her. You know how women are. At least Louise was better. She wasn't nearly as annoying. She got pregnant too. If she hadn't gone to Colorado Springs, I might have stayed with her."

A chorus of footsteps sounds outside the room, and Sheriff Winstanley calls out to Ron, telling him to open the door. Michael looks at the door as it opens, then steals a glance at Johns. Johns smiles a knowing smile. Sheriff Winstanley enters the room, carrying handcuffs.

"Michael Delaney, you're under arrest."

Michael stands, looking at him with raised hands. "On what charge?"

"Impersonating an officer of the law."

The sheriff comes forward, but Michael steps back.

"Wait, he just confessed to me. He just admitted he murdered his wife."

Winstanley ignores him and steps forward, grabbing Michael by the arm. Michael spins away and raises his pistol, aiming it at Johns. But before he can fire, the sheriff chops down with his arm, knocking the pistol to the ground. Ron and the sheriff wrestle Michael to the ground and pin his arms behind his back while slapping on the cuffs. Michael sees the pistol resting at Johns's feet, but he's surprised that Johns doesn't try to pick it up. He could easily use it to shoot the three of them and walk out. Instead, he sits calmly, watching as they raise Michael to his feet.

"You're going to jail," the sheriff says to Michael, pushing him toward the door. Michael looks back and sees Johns smirk and wave one of his shackled hands.

Chapter 45

Louise

The automobile stops, and the driver looks back at me sitting beside Jacob.

"Sixty-seven Garfield Street, ma'am."

I look at the two-story brick house and nod. He opens his door, steps down to the road, then opens the door for me.

"Come on, honey," I say to Jacob, taking him by the hand and stepping down. The driver carries the bag to the bottom of the steps and waits. I hand him a quarter, and he tips his hat, thanking me, and walks back to his automobile.

Standing at the bottom of the steps, I pause and take a deep breath. Jacob looks up at me, his little hand in mine. Holding our bag in my other hand, we struggle our way to the top of the stairs and ring the bell. I turn around and survey the area. A park is on the opposite side of the street, and the streetlamps have turned on. It's an early summer evening, and the crickets are chirping all around us. I hear a noise from behind the door and turn around, wondering who might open it.

The door opens, and John McKenna stands looking at me. A curious look on his face. After a brief moment, recognition dawns, and his eyebrows lift in surprise.

"Hello, John."

"Louise."

We stand awkwardly, looking at each other, before he invites me in. I struggle with the bag, and he takes it from me, looking down at Jacob. He shuts the door behind us, placing the bag on the rug in the entry.

"John?" I hear a familiar voice call from the back. "Who is it?"

He looks at me and smiles.

"Come and see," he calls out. "You'll never guess."

I hear footsteps at the back of the house. Then she appears in the hallway. She's heavier than the last time I saw her, but all the weight is in the front. Of course, she's the type to gain all her weight in her belly and nowhere else. Her limbs are still as lean as ever.

"Louise?" she says, rushing forward.

"Hi, Barbara."

She reaches me, and we hug, laughing. I release Jacob's hand, and he burrows into my dress, curious and afraid of these new strangers. When Barbara and I release each other, I bend down to talk to him.

"Jacob, this is your aunt Barbara and your uncle John."

He looks at me with wide eyes, then holds out his arms. I pick him up and stand.

"Come in, come in," Barbara says, putting an arm around me.

We walk to the couch in their front room, two sisters carrying babies. She has one still inside her. Mine is two and getting bigger every day.

"How old is he?" Barbara asks.

"Two."

"Is this your first?" I ask, pointing to her belly. We've reached the couch now and sit beside each other holding hands. John sits on the chair opposite us. Jacob remains in my lap.

"It is," she says, smiling and looking at John. It's a look of admiration, of love. She turns back to me, and we stare at each other. It's been almost three years. I'm sure she's got a million questions, and I have some myself. But neither of us seems to know where to start.

"I missed you," I say. "I'm sorry."

She shakes her head, tears welling up in her eyes. "I'm sorry too."

Thirty minutes later, we're still seated on the couch. John went to the kitchen to get us drinks. Jacob lies on the couch beside me, sleeping. She told me about her wedding to John, about our parents, and what names they've considered for their baby. I told her about Charles and my life with him, about my time in Denver, and about meeting Michael on the train. She shook her head multiple times and reached out and hugged me. We were never close when we were kids. But now, sitting together, I realize my blame for that. I spent too much time being jealous of her, not loving her.

"I'm sorry I missed your wedding," I tell her.

"Me too. I wish you'd been there."

I look down at my hands in my lap. "I was stupid."

"Louise, I'm not Mother. You don't have to say anything like that to me. I'm just glad you're home."

I look up at her, and tears fill our eyes. We fall silent, and I know we've come to the part in the conversation I've been dreading. Michael was right; I have to face Charles.

"I need to ask you something," I say.

"Yes."

I hesitate.

"What?"

"I need to go back. I need to make sure Charles can't ever get Jacob."

"What? Why?"

I told her about the new hotel owner's death.

"If I don't go, he'll be out. I'll never be safe. I'll never be able to live here again."

She nods, the weight of my words hitting her. "What do you need from me?"

I look over at Jacob, who is sleeping on the couch beside me. "Will you take him? Keep him safe?"

She looks into my eyes. "Of course. How long?"

"I'm not sure."

Chapter 46

Michael

Michael lies on the bed in his jail cell, looking up at the unfinished ceiling. Exposed pipes and wires cover the area separating the prisoners from the free folk. Occasionally, he can hear movement from above, the free world. He always knew this was a possibility. That someday he could find himself in a jail cell. Admittedly, he figured it would be because he had killed the man in the cell next to him, not because he'd been found out.

He swings his legs off the edge of the bed, stands, and paces back and forth. Since being arrested, he's spent 90 percent of his time in this cell. A man was brought in yesterday for public intoxication. He was assigned to the cell on Michael's right. The man said he didn't remember, but he was accused of taking a swing at a couple of police officers. He was released earlier this morning. Now, it's just Michael and Johns in this area of the jail.

After walking back and forth fifty times in his small, cramped quarters, he sits down and picks up the book he had selected. Yesterday, Ron, the jailer, had come around offering books. He said the community had donated them to the jailhouse a few months back, but most were borrowed by other inmates or ruined. Michael had two options: *The Adventures of Huckleberry Finn* or *Pride and Prejudice*. He chose the latter. Ron smiled when he selected it.

"Lover boy, huh?"

Michael shrugged. "I've read *Huckleberry Finn* before."

He opens the book and flips to Chapter Two, having finished Chapter One yesterday. He's never considered himself much of a reader, and Chapter One did little to change that. It was all about a family of young women eager to marry in Victorian-age England when a rich newcomer, Mr. Bingley, buys a house in their neighborhood.

After reading only a few lines, he hears movement on the bunk next to him. Since his arrest, Johns hadn't spoken to him. Now he walks to the bars that separate them.

"I've read it," he says.

Michael watches him. "And?"

"Entertaining. Some unexpected twists. Great character development. Makes me glad I was never born at that time in England."

Michael says nothing, curious why Johns is speaking to him now.

"How did you know?" Michael asks.

"What? That you were no longer a threat?"

"Yeah?"

"I talked to the sheriff."

Michael narrows his eyes as he looks at him. "You told him?"

Johns nods.

"How did you know?"

"Ah," he said, shrugging, "I knew from the first time you came in here. You were too nervous, jittery." Johns shakes his hands to exaggerate the movement. "I could tell you didn't belong. Plus, you looked familiar."

"Why didn't you tell the sheriff after the first time we talked?"

"I was curious. I wanted to learn your motive. See what you'd do. After the second meeting, the intrigue was gone for me. I called for the sheriff and told him. He was just waiting for you to come back."

Michael rests against the exterior wall.

"Why confess to me?"

Johns turns his head to the side as if he's considering the question. "I don't know. I guess it was, as I said, you were no longer a threat. And," he pauses, then smiles, "I felt sorry for you. I decided I'd throw you a bone. End the mystery."

Michael feels a loathing stronger than any he can remember. "You were wrong, you know."

"Oh?"

"She was pregnant."

"Who? Louise? Of course, she was."

Michael shakes his head. "No, not Louise. Helen."

Johns tries to hide it, but Michael sees the flash of anger in the blue eyes.

"After her body was found, they performed an autopsy. She was two months pregnant with your child." Michael closes the book on his lap and crosses his arms, closing his eyes. "Ironic, huh? You killed her because you found her useless. Couldn't bear you an heir. But you killed her and him."

Michael opens his left eye and sees Johns clenching and unclenching his jaw. Finally, after a beat, he speaks.

"It's okay. I have another."

"True, but you don't know where he is."

"He's with his mother." He said it as if it were common knowledge. "I don't know if she has yet. But someday soon, she's going to go home to Chicago. And when she does, my guy will be waiting for her."

Chapter 47

Louise

The train comes to a stop at the Kansas City station, and I keep my head down as I walk past the man who's been stalking me since Chicago. While at Barbara's house, I looked out the window and saw him. He hasn't changed much, other than packing on some additional weight. It's the same man who had stood under the pecan tree in Austin. The same one who had followed Charles to the park when he confronted me about leaving. He's tried to disguise himself by shaving his mustache, but I know it's him. I'd recognize his shoulder stoop anywhere.

I descend the stairs of the train and walk briskly through the station. I fight the urge to look back as I walk, knowing I'm moving fast, unencumbered by a big bag and toddler. I reach the women's lavatory at the edge of the station and enter, stealing a glance over my shoulder. He's there, hiding around the corner, trying to stay out of sight. I open the door and walk through the room, passing two stalls and a row of sinks. A woman occupies one stall, only her feet visible. Another examines herself in the mirror at the sink. She sees me pass by in the mirror, but I don't acknowledge her on the way to the window. I put down my bag, pry open the window, and push my small bag out to the other side. Preparing to climb out, I look over and see her watching me. I realize enlisting her as an ally will be more beneficial than an informant.

"There's a man out there following me," I explain.

She says nothing, watching me.

"Please help me."

Her face softens, and an understanding passes between us. She nods, and I turn back to the window, squeeze through the opening, and drop to the other side. I scrape my shin across the metal surface of the window frame in my fall and gasp. I kneel on the grass; a large bush covers my existence from passersby as I examine my wound. I see a movement and look up. She waves me away with her hand, mouthing "go," and shuts the window. I pick up my bag and walk away, checking over my shoulder. To my right, I see a group of bushes and duck behind them, making sure nobody sees me. After several minutes, longer than I would have guessed, the stalker exits the station, looking around frantically. Assuming I've taken a carriage or automobile into the city, he hires one and moves off. Once he's safely out of sight, I exit the bushes.

An hour later, I walk into the city hall on the Missouri side. While riding on the train with Michael, he had told me the names of all the people he had spoken with during his investigation. A short, husky man with a bright smile holds the door open as I approach. I thank him and enter as he leaves. After navigating my way to the mayor's office, I walk in and am greeted by a man seated behind a desk. He holds a pen and appears to be writing something.

"Can I help you, miss?"

"Yes, I'd like to talk with Mayor Brown, please?"

"I'm sorry, but the mayor isn't in. You just missed him."

I look over at the wall and see the mayor's picture.

"Is that him?" I ask.

"Yes."

"Thank you," I call out, exiting.

I rush down the hallway and burst out of the exit. I stand on the steps of the building and look in either direction. Several hundred feet to my right, I see him. I take off down the steps. When I get within ten feet, he hears my footsteps and turns around, eyeing me curiously.

"Mr. Mayor?" I say, out of breath.

"Yes?"

"May I talk with you?"

He looks down at his watch. "I'm sorry, but I have an engagement I'm late for."

"Please, sir, it's very important."

He checks his watch again, then looks back into my eyes. "I can give you five minutes." We're standing in front of a church, and he motions to the steps leading up to the front door. I join him on the middle stair. He sets down his bag and looks at me. "How can I help?"

"It's about a prisoner you hold in the jail, Mr. Johns."

He raises an eyebrow. "What about him?"

"I knew him as Charles Watson and Richard Amhurst. He's my husband and the father of my child."

Mayor Brown's eyes go wide with surprise.

"He's a very dangerous man, sir. He killed his first wife, and he tried to kill me as well. I was lucky enough to escape him. But I know if he's released from jail, he'll not rest until he has me and my child."

The mayor exhales a large breath and looks out at the people walking by. "What's your name?"

□"Louise."

"Louise," he says, leaning forward. "Not Barbara?"

I duck my head. "That was the name I went by."

He nods. "Your husband is being released from jail tomorrow."

"What?" I cry.

He holds up a hand. "The man who accused him of fraud is dead. His trial was supposed to be next week, but with nobody to stand against him, we have nothing to try him for. The victim is gone." He pauses, letting his words sink in. "There was another man who came to us with allegations against him. He claimed to be a detective from Denver, but it turns out he lied. He's not a detective at all. He's never worked for the Denver police. They've never heard of him."

My head spins, and I realize I'm holding my breath. *Michael isn't really a detective? Who is he then?* I lean forward, putting my head in my hands.

He puts a hand on my shoulder. "Do you have any proof of what your husband's done? Any proof at all that he's the man who killed this other woman? Any proof that he tried to kill you?"

I bring my hands to my lap and think about the question. There must be something. I think of his victims. There was his first wife, then the girl he had dated before me in Austin, Mary Tuberville. Two other victims spring to my mind. He killed his aunt and uncle, I'm sure of it. Maybe the Colorado Springs police have something. I could reach out to them. Go there and talk to them. But then what? In the meantime, he will be released from jail. He'll go after Jacob. I can't let that happen.

The mayor watches me and knows the answer to his question without me responding. "I'm sorry, Louise. But there's one other problem."

"What?"

"Your name."

"My name?"

"Yes. What is it? Louise? Or Barbara? You see, in either case, if you accuse your husband, the defense attorney is going to attack your credibility. You've used different names and even married him with a fake name." He shakes his head. "I'm sorry. I recommend you talk to the police where you are. See if they can help protect you. I have no doubt what you say is true, I just can't do anything for you. We've held him as long as we can, and he'll be released tomorrow."

Chapter 48

Louise

I place the cowboy hat on my head, look in the mirror one last time, and leave my hotel room. This is the first time I've ever worn cowboy boots, and they feel hard and restrictive. I should have put them on yesterday after buying them, but I was too busy. Along with the cowboy boots and hat, I bought jeans, a belt buckle, and a flannel shirt. The jeans and shirt are larger than they should be. My hope is they will mask my female figure.

After dawning the clothing, minus the hat, I pulled out a pair of sharp scissors and cut off the long, dark hair I've had as long as I can remember. I shaped the hair to look as masculine as possible. I wonder how long it will take to grow back. The last touch, before the cowboy hat, was applying the fake mustache. It wasn't because it looked genuine. Anyone with a clear view of my face would see it wasn't mine. The point was to obstruct a full view of my face and a bandana was too much.

Once I'm out of the hotel, I walk two blocks to the courthouse and wait. The mayor said he'd be released from jail at nine a.m., and I've arrived twenty minutes early, just in case. I stand across the street, the leather pouch slung over my shoulder, tapping my foot. I'm not sure how today will go. I'm not even sure I'll survive it, but I have no choice. This is a step I have to take.

At two minutes past nine, I see the front doors open, and Richard exits. He stops at the top of the stairs, takes a big breath, and looks around like he's the king of the world. It's a beautiful, warm, late-summer day, and I'm sure he's enjoying the fresh air and sunlight. He moves down the steps and walks along the road, his head up, enjoying his newfound freedom. I follow on the opposite side of the road, back several steps so he can't see me keeping pace.

After several blocks, he turns into Mill Creek Park and sits on a park bench. Another man I recognize joins him, and they converse. I can see that the other man is doing most of the talking. Richard remains calm, watching him. Finally, they stand, and Richard pats him on the shoulder. They part, and I keep my focus on Richard. He walks several more blocks and reaches the Kansas City railway station, a place I know well. He walks in, carrying no luggage, and enters the ticket line. I stay back but close enough to see the departure board. I don't have to hear him to know where he's going. One line on the board says everything: Chicago 10:30 a.m. He's going after our son.

He buys his ticket, looks at his watch, then scans the station. He sees what he needs and walks toward it. I take a breath and realize the time has come. I follow him as he reaches the hallway and enters the men's lavatory. Thankfully, the hallway is empty. I unlatch the buckle on the satchel, remove the pistol, pull back the hammer, and push open the door. He stands at the urinal in the middle of the room. I walk up behind him, put the gun to the back of his head, and whisper, "His life isn't your life." He startles and starts to turn when I pull the trigger. The sound reverberates in the small lavatory like a cannon in a narrow canyon. Blood sprays the wall. I feel it cover my face as he slumps against the urinal and falls to the ground.

I spin around, walk out the door, and duck into the ladies' room next door. Thankfully, the room is empty. I walk to one of the two stalls, open the door, wipe my face with my sleeve, and begin undressing. I open my satchel, remove my dress, and put it on. I change my shoes, put on lipstick the best I can without a mirror, rub some rouge on my cheeks, put the men's clothes in the satchel, and exit the stall.

Someone pulls the exit door open momentarily, and I catch a glimpse of the crowd that has gathered in the hallway. I move to the sink, wash any visible signs of Richard's blood from me, and look at myself in the mirror. I can see my lower lip is trembling, but I can't worry about that now. I have more to do. I consider my next step. Do I exit through the door or the window? If I choose the door, they may stop everyone who walks past. People will see me and possibly remember me. If I exit through the window, I run the risk of being seen. A woman climbing through the window of a murder scene is highly suspicious. But then I remember the large bush that covers the area in front of the window.

I make up my mind, place the satchel at the bottom of the garbage can, and head for the window. I open it, climb out, being sure to keep my leg off the frame, and fall to the ground. I look through the branches of the bush and see nobody watching me. I walk briskly across the front of the station and begin putting distance between me and the body of the man who has tormented me for years.

Chapter 49

Michael

Michael lies on the bed in his jail cell, frustrated and angry. Yesterday, he was arraigned in front of a judge for the crime of impersonating a police officer. His frustration isn't that he thinks he's innocent. He knows he isn't. He pleaded guilty and was sentenced to six months in jail. Six months he would be here. Six months his former cell neighbor, real name Thomas Slater, would be out free. What eats him up inside is that he told Louise to go home to Chicago. He asked her to see her mother, and Slater had someone waiting for her. Now, no doubt, Slater has Jacob.

He looks around the jail cell and wonders how he might escape. He stands, walks to the cell bars, and tugs on each one, hoping and praying one might give way. After trying each one, he sits back on the bed. There's no way he's breaking out of here. His only hope might be the next time he's taken out of the cell. Often, it's only Frank who escorts him to the shower. The next time Frank comes, he'll test. See what he can do. If he has to steal a gun and threaten him, he will. He's got to get to Louise before it's too late.

Punching his fist into the bed, he picks up the book lying next to him and begins to read. Elizabeth Bennett, the heroine of the story, is infatuated with the soldier Mr. Wickham. Mr. Bingley and Mr. Darcy have gone away, and Whickham is confirming her belief that Mr. Darcy is the root of all evil.

Twenty minutes into his reading, he hears Frank, the jailer, coming down the row of cells. Several prisoners call out to him, complaining that they need water or aren't feeling well. All excuses to break up the monotony of incarceration. Frank walks past them as if he doesn't hear. Michael lays stretched out on his bed, legs crossed at the ankles, the book in his hands.

"Delaney," Frank calls, smacking his keys against the iron bars.

Michael drops the book so he can look at him.

"You have a visitor," Frank says, smiling.

Michael places the book down, making sure to keep his spot. He stands and walks toward the front of the cell, perplexed. Nobody he knows realizes he's here. Frank opens the cell and instructs Michael to extend his wrists. He considers taking a chance now. Striking Frank, stealing his gun and keys, making a break for it. But the news of a mysterious visitor gives him pause.

He extends his arms, and Frank slaps the cuffs on each wrist before pushing him forward. Michael walks through the row of cells with Frank at his back.

"Didn't realize you were married," Frank says to him.

Michael frowns, wondering if he's being teased.

"Young and pretty. What a body, too. I like a woman with some shape to her."

They reach the door where Michael had spoken to Johns each time he came. Frank opens the door and pushes Michael inside. The room's empty, and Michael looks back at Frank.

"Sit down. She'll be here in a minute. Ron's bringing her. I think he likes her, too."

Michael walks around the table and sits so his back is to the stone wall and he faces the door. Frank stays on the other side of the room. He has a faraway look in his eye as he leans against the wall, his gut sticking out. "My only complaint is her hair. Why does she keep it so short? Is that your fault? You don't want other men looking?"

Michael glares at him, wondering who he could be talking about.

Footsteps sound outside the door and it opens. Michael locks eyes with the familiar woman standing in the opening.

Frank greets her, steps forward, pulls out a chair, and steps back.

The woman thanks him, sits down, and looks across the table at Michael. Neither says anything, and Frank goes back to leaning on the wall. The woman turns around to look at him.

"Sir, I'd like to speak with my husband alone, please."

"I'm sorry, ma'am. He's dangerous, attacked the sheriff. He can't be left alone."

The woman turns and looks back at Michael, then to Frank. When she speaks, it's hard and cold.

"I think I know my husband, sir. Now leave us, or do I have to talk to the sheriff again?"

Frank sighs and leaves the room, muttering. Before closing the door, he says, "I'll be right outside."

A million questions run through Michael's head as he and Louise stare at each other.

"Surprised to see me?"

"Your husband?" Michael says. "He's got a man. They knew you were in Chicago."

"I know," she says without concern.

"But?"

She shakes her head. "He can no longer hurt us." She pauses and places her hand on the table. "You were right, you know."

"I was? About what?"

"About him and me. He was never going to stop. You said I would never feel completely safe, and you were right."

Michael watches her. "I didn't mean..."

"It was the only way. The man who followed me in Austin followed me to Chicago. He met with him here in Kansas City. He knew. He bought a ticket to Chicago. He was going for Jacob. I couldn't let that happen."

Michael swallows, feeling a mixture of relief and guilt.

"I had to come and tell you."

"Thank you."

She nods. "There's something I want to know, though."

"What?"

"Why were you looking for him? Who are you? I know now you're not a detective. He didn't know you. How did you know him?"

Michael looks down at his shackled hands. "Helen was my sister."

"Your sister?"

"She was much younger. I was long gone by the time she met him. He seduced her and got her to run away with him. A story very similar to yours. Our mother agonized over her. She blamed herself. Thought it was something she did wrong in raising her. She tried to find her but couldn't. When the news came that they had found her body in a field in Denver, it broke her heart. I'll never forget taking her to claim the body. The torture was palpable. She was her only daughter. She loved her so much."

Michael looks across the table at Louise.

"Afterward, she fell ill. She couldn't get out of bed. Three weeks later, she was dead. An hour before she died, I was with her. Her heart was broken. She had nothing left, but suddenly she gripped my hand. She asked me to find Thomas and bring him to justice. I promised her I would. I searched for him. I learned he was seen coming east from Denver. I followed his trail to Kansas City. Someone he knew in business said he was in jail for fraud. I visited the mayor and the sheriff. When I was introduced to him, I knew."

Michael sighs.

"I debated on what to do. I thought about killing him right then. But I knew my mother wouldn't want that. I thought I could get him legally. Make him pay that way. That's why the last couple of days have been so hard. It's not just because I get such lovely accommodations." He raises his hands to point out the décor. "I felt like I failed. I failed my mother, Helen, and you. I sat in here, powerless to stop him. You don't know the relief you've brought to me."

Michael reaches across the table. Louise puts her hand in his.

"You don't need to tell me anything more. I don't want to know. But there is something I need from you," he says.

"Anything."

"Your mother loves you. Go home to her."

Chapter 50

Louise

I stand at the bottom of the steps of my childhood home, preparing to enter. Almost three years ago I had stood in this very spot, anticipating with trepidation the ensuing interaction. I was returning home from my first year of college in disgrace. Earlier in the week, I had been expelled from the university. After being bullied by my roommate for months, I snapped and threw all her clothes out the window. She retaliated by stealing my paper, copying it, and turning it in as her own to the professor. The two of them colluded to remove me. I wondered if my parents knew. If they had received word from the dean. I worried about what they might say, never believing my side of things. How angry they would be. When Barbara and I walked into the house, they greeted us as if nothing had happened. They didn't know, and I had time to craft a narrative. A story I never told.

I feel the same trepidation now, but for different reasons. I no longer want secrets. There's much they know already. I left home because I was pregnant with Charles's baby. I chased after him and found him. That I now have a son. Barbara might have told them more; it doesn't really matter. Now, I'll tell them everything they want to know. I'll hide nothing.

I take a deep breath, square my shoulders, and walk up the steps. When the train had docked at the station, I went to Barbara's house. I needed to see my son, hold him in my arms, and know without a doubt he was mine. His father would never take him from me. But they weren't home, having come here to visit my parents. I considered staying at Barbara's. Waiting until they returned. But the longing for Jacob, and the knowledge I was delaying the ensuing confrontation, pushed my feet into motion.

I extend my hand to knock, but before I do, the door opens. Only the glass screen door is between me and my mother. We look at each other, reading body language. She's aged, the lines around her mouth more pronounced, the gray in her hair more abundant. The time since I left has been hard on her.

"Hello, Mother," I say, bracing my feet and preparing for whatever might come my way.

She pushes open the screen door and rushes at me. She throws her arms around me in a sweeping embrace. On the train from Kansas City, I had imagined this moment over and over. In each iteration, I never expected this.

I stand awkwardly. My arms are at my side as my mother clings to me like a raft in a waterfall. After several seconds, she stands back and looks at me. What I see is even more shocking. Tears brim her eyelids. I can't remember ever seeing her cry about me. She grips my face with her hands, bringing it close to hers.

"Louise," she says, the tears now spilling over and running down her cheeks, "can you forgive me?"

It's not shock I feel but bewilderment. I couldn't speak if I wanted to. I stare at her, my mouth open. I don't know how much time passes. It's as if time stands still. Finally, she takes me by the hand and leads me to the steps. She sits, pulling me down beside her, our hips and shoulders touching. She looks at me and leans her head against my shoulder, grabbing my hand and holding it with both of hers. She looks back up in my eyes and I frown.

"Forgive you for what?"

She shakes her head. "I should have told you."

"Told me what?"

She looks away, still gripping my hand. "There's something you need to understand. Something that I've never told you before."

"Okay."

She grips my hand tighter and turns to face the road. "Before your father, I fell for a man. He was older and very handsome. When I saw Charles at that theater, I couldn't believe it. He looked so much like that man I knew. Even his mannerisms, the way he carried himself. He was bold, like Charles, confident. I fell head over heels for him. One day, he convinced me to meet him down by the docks, unchaperoned."

She looks at me. "That was something a girl just didn't do. It was dangerous and exciting and I knew I shouldn't, but I agreed. It was improper, but I liked it. I walked home that night, daydreaming of him. But as I lay in bed, trying to sleep, reality struck. I realized there was no future with him. He was a man who would never be what I needed. He lacked ambition. He wasn't what I wanted."

She stops and looks back at the road.

"The night Charles came to dinner; I saw you two. I saw the way you looked at him. I wasn't surprised. He was handsome and desirable. But what concerned me was what I saw from him. He wanted you. The attraction was unmistakable. You were his prey. I wanted to warn you, but worried that if I did, I'd push you right into his arms. I kept silent, hoping you'd see the light like I did."

Tears fill her eyes again as she looks at me.

"I'm so sorry, Louise. I'm your mother, and I should have protected you. I should have warned you."

"Mom, it's not your fault. I slept with him. I chased him. I was a headstrong girl who wouldn't have listened if you had warned me. It was my fault, not yours."

She puts her arm around my shoulders, and I wrap mine around her waist.

"Honey, I'll never ask you, and you never have to tell me what happened to him. I'm just so happy to have you back."

We sit there holding each other, and I clear my throat. "There's something I need to tell you."

She doesn't look at me. "I told you, I don't want to know."

"It's not that."

She leans back away from me. "What is it?"

I look down, unable to look her in the eyes. "I was kicked out of school."

She looks away from me and smiles. "I know."

"You knew?"

"A letter came."

"The dean said he wouldn't send it."

She shrugs. "He lied."

"You weren't mad?"

"Oh, I was furious. But I was waiting to talk to you about it. I didn't want to ruin your first week home, and then your aunt died..."

I looked away from her, shaking my head. "I was so afraid to tell you."

She reaches out and guides my face back to her. We look into each other's eyes.

"Louise, did you ever wonder why I was so hard on you?"

I chuckle. "Every day."

She smiles. "You were the one. I love Barbara, and she's wonderful. But I knew how much you were capable of. I knew how smart and tenacious you could be. There was nothing you couldn't do. Honey, I pushed you because I loved you. I'm sorry that you felt I pushed too hard. There are so many things I wish I could redo. But hear me now—you will do great things in this world."

I kiss her cheek, tears streaming down my face.

An hour later, I walk up the grand staircase and stop outside my bedroom door. Inside, I can hear my mother reading a bedtime story to Jacob. When he saw me come home, he ran to me and hugged me. For five minutes, he wouldn't let me go, and I loved it. It makes me wonder, how can something so beautiful and loving come from someone so bad? Jacob is sweet and kind. His father was cruel and selfish. The thought makes me think of my father. After we walked into the house and Jacob greeted me, Barbara and John came forward, but my father was strangely absent. Mother, seeing my concern, broke the news. Father had died of a heart attack a year after my disappearance. She said he never got over me leaving. He hired an investigator to find me but never did. They thought I was in Houston because that's where they thought Charles was from. They couldn't find any trace of me or him. Charles and I were gone, with no clues about how to find us. Mother won't say it, and I won't force her. But my leaving was a betrayal for him.

Not wanting to interrupt, I cross the hall and open the door to the sewing room. There's one more soul in the house I haven't greeted since arriving. I pull back the sheet and look inside the cage.

"Peekaboo," Nibbles says as he looks at me.

I laugh, and he mimics my laugh as I open the cage. He climbs off his perch, steps onto my finger, and climbs up my arm. Standing on my shoulder, he looks at me and repeats the phrase one more time, and I realize once again that I've been loved my whole life. I just took it for granted.

I look at the doorframe and see my mother there. "He still knows you."

I smile. "I guess he does."

She comes to me and extends her finger. Nibbles steps off my shoulder and goes to her.

"Jacob wants to say goodnight."

I nod, cross the hall, and enter my childhood room. Everything is the same, just as I had left it. The only difference is my son lies in my bed. I walk to him, and he reaches up for me. I hug him and kiss his head, then lay beside him as he falls to sleep. With my hand brushing his hair, a thought comes to me. Am I no better than his father?

Richard was evil. He killed multiple people, including his wife and his aunt and uncle. He would have killed me if I hadn't escaped. He wanted our son. He wanted a puppet he could mold and control. Had I not done what I did, what would have become of Jacob? Would he turn out just like his father? How many more lives would Richard have taken?

Before I left Kansas City, I donated the money I had stolen from Richard. Thirty thousand dollars given to an orphanage. The only thing I wanted from him was beside me.

I look down and see Jacob's long eyelashes, the ones he inherited from me. I would have done anything to protect my son and I'll spend the rest of my life making sure his life is everything it should be. I can't go back and change the past. Richard's blood will always stain my skin. But I can alter the future. I can raise our son the right way. I can show him the love he deserves.

It makes me realize; *Oh, how desperate one life can be.*

Also by

D.J. Maughan

Vanished From Budapest
Book one of the Vanished Series

Two graduate students fall in love; one goes missing....

In the year 2000, Peter Andrassy is heartbroken by the murder of his wife. Widowed for a year and hoping to mend his broken heart, the former NYC detective has returned to his home country of Hungary to work as a private investigator when he's contacted by an American graduate student who is desperate to find his missing British girlfriend.

A gifted interrogator, Peter senses the boyfriend is intentionally withholding information. Could it be related to sex trafficking? Young women, often foreign, disappear daily in the capital city, never to be seen again. The clock is ticking, and the case is growing cold.

Can Peter find Samantha before it's too late?
https://www.amazon.com/dp/B0BPNCQ3P8

About the author

D.J. Maughan is an avid reader, event manager, father, husband, public speaker, and award-winning author. His debut series, Vanished, is based in Budapest, Hungary. As a young man, he lived in Budapest and now enjoys returning to the city that helped shape him. He seeks inspiration everywhere, especially while studying and visiting diverse places and cultures. Whether jumping from a cliff in Hawaii or hiking the Plitvica Lakes in Croatia, he's in heaven as long as his wife and four sons are at his side.

Acknowledgements

Thank you to my beta readers. Your insights helped shape this novel. Brooke Maughan, Lupe Merino, Laurie Clark, Luke Barber, Matt Young, Jerry Paskett, Jim Thomas, Paul Gyorka, Kari Garrett, Laura Martin, and Mya Merino.

Much gratitude to my editor, Jonathan Starke. Thank you for continually teaching me.